WEESQUACHAK

AND THE LOST ONES

WEESQUACHAK

AND THE LOST ONES

Ruby Slipperjack

Theytus Books Ltd.
Penticton, BC

Canadian Cataloguing in Publication Data

Slipperjack, Ruby, 1952-
  Weesquachak and the lost ones
  ISBN 0-919441-88-2
  I. Title.
PS8587.L53S43 2000   C813'.54C00-910366-X
PR9199.3.S55123W43 2000

Cover Art: Ruby Slipperjack
Editorial: Greg Young-Ing
Book Design & Layout: Florene Belmore
Special Thanks: Regina Gabriel

The publisher gratefully acknowledges the support of The Canada Council for
the Arts, Department of Canadian Heritage and the British Columbia Arts
Council in the publication of this book.

Published by Theytus Books Ltd., Penticton BC

Printed and bound in Canada

CHAPTER 1

My suitcases were on the ground on each side of me. This was as good a place as any to rest. From the hill where I stood, I looked around at the quiet stillness of the morning. The lake lay dark along the bay and melted into a steely grey along the horizon past the island. The sky was heavy with low grey clouds and a few flies fluttered over the dead flowers and bushes. It was the end of September and everything had pretty much ended.

The sea-gulls were ready to fly south and I too was on my way south to the city in search of a job. I was going to find a job! I had said that with such confidence but in all truth, all I had was a high school diploma. I wasn't proud of that though, because I knew that I couldn't even do grade eleven math. They had just passed me along and no one cared if I could actually do things at that grade level. Oh, I hated high school! A large raven swooped over my head, emitting a loud squawk as if he too agreed with me. Stupid bird, what does he know anyway!

It was 1972. I was nineteen years old and I felt trapped in my life. I was suffocating! But, I was on my way to find out what I could do for myself. Dad was starting to have that worried look on his face as if he had just discovered he had another mouth to feed. I knew it would soon occur to him to find me a husband as quick as he could to get me out of the house. Well, I hung around as long as I could. I had no where else to go. When I graduated from high school last summer, I got a summer job in the city and came home in the fall just when everyone was headed to the trap-lines. My sister-in-law seemed so pleased to see me that it didn't take long to figure out that she was pregnant and desperately needed an extra pair of hands. So, I used my savings to buy all the things that I would need out

5

there, like hand-cream, toothpaste and deodorant, and spent the winter out at the trap-line with my brother and his wife. We came back in late May and the baby was born a few days later. That was too close! It occurred to me then that she could very well have had the baby earlier when we were still in the bush. What help could I have been then? I stayed around at the community until the end of June and then I lived with my sister and her family in Nipigon for the summer.

I arrived here at the end of August and I was asked, "Who are you going to marry? Who are you going to marry?" so many times that I finally answered, just that once, and said, "The Pope." It might have been funny I suppose, but it was the Priest who was asking. Every time I stayed somewhere for more than a month, the guessing and speculation would start and then the rumours would begin about why a young woman could possibly be just drifting around. I smiled and heaved a big sigh. There was never an end to that. There's that raven over my head again, what does he want with me? Stupid thing.

I picked up my suitcases and continued on my way past the creek and to the path along the railroad tracks. I paused and looked down one of the many trails that veered off to the lake. I could hear someone running towards me. I continued walking and then I heard Ron calling and soon he fell into step beside me. I glanced at him, he looked like he had just got out of bed. His hair was sticking out all over the place, a matted bed-head. I had heard his girlfriend from another town had moved in with him. His parents were bragging about Ron's new girlfriend at Mother's place the other day. It was supposed to make me feel bad. I smiled.

"How did you know I was leaving?" I asked.

"Oh, I got up to go to the toilet and saw you standing there on the hill."

I felt my face go red. He always had a way of embarrassing me! What did he go and say that for? He was about as sophisticated as a piece of driftwood. No, that was an insult to the driftwood. I didn't say anything else as I continued walking. He said nothing more either until we came to the shim-shack where he suddenly pulled me to a stop. With a smile, he gave me a big hug and whispered, "c.b.t.m. Janine." Then he was gone. It was a short form he began using when we were teenagers so other people by the station wouldn't understand. It stood for, "come back to me, Janine." I giggled as I watched him disappear back down the path. He always said that every time I left for school. I smiled as I walked on. This time I wasn't going to school. And, maybe I would not be coming back.

They forgot about me. Their children have never even heard of me. The adults don't remember anymore. The old have no one to listen but I... I will not be forgotten! I will make them know that I still exist. I will make them get to know me again. I exist. I am here, always have been—right among them. Now, I've been watching this girl. She comes and goes and doesn't seem to know what she is supposed to do. She seems lost. I saw her coming out of the cabin this morning. Good looking girl. Interesting... but I don't think she likes me. Maybe she doesn't like ravens. Hmmm, perhaps she likes me better soft and quiet.

I continued down the path to the C.N. Railway stop. We had long since stopped calling it a station since it was no longer a station as such, but more like an open shack. Strange, but there was that black and white dog again. It meets me when I get off the train and it comes to meet me when I get back on the train. I put my heavy suitcases down and reached to scratch the dog's head. Yes, yes, my welcoming committee and my last farewell. I didn't know whose dog he was. Strange, that. I once used to know the name of every dog in the community and the few cats there were. My hand came away gritty. Yuck! I patted his head. He walked me to the train stop and sat down beside my suitcases. There was absolutely no one around.

There were a few dogs barking somewhere by the shoreline. Soon, the postal clerk showed up with the morning's mail bag. Nothing much passed between us, other than a nod. We waited as the distant hum of the coming train became louder. Soon, the train came to a hissing stop and I brushed the top of the dog's head one last time and picked up my suitcases. I boarded the train determined that I would not be coming back again.

It was mid-afternoon when I got off at Sioux Lookout, Ontario. It was beginning to rain. I walked briskly across the cold parking lot and across the street to the Sioux Hotel. After paying for a room, I lugged my suitcases up the stairs and down the hall to the room at the end. Just as I turned the key, I heard a voice across the hall that sounded just like Fred. It couldn't be. He should be at his trap-line by now. I entered the room and made a bee-line for the tub.

When I was up to my neck in warm water, I heard Fred's voice again from one of the rooms. Freddy...

I happened to be on my way to the store in June when I noticed a baseball game going on in the field by the railway tracks. I sat on the store window sill with several other ladies and watched the game for a while when I noticed Freddy among them. I had heard that his wife had died in a car accident last year. I never heard if they had any children. Now, there he was looking so handsome in his t-shirt. I could hear him laughing from there. Then, during a break he came running toward the store and his face lit up when he noticed me. I got very shy for some reason. He walked right up to me and gave me two dollars saying, "Get two pop for me, I'll come and get them in a while." He turned and ran back to the field. Just then, I became aware that the ladies were giggling and whispering together. I knew it really looked like Fred and I were that familiar with each other that he would come up to me like that and ask me to get something for him. I had not seen him for several years and, oh, I was so embarrassed! I went into the store though, and bought the pop, and sat them down beside me at the window sill and watched the rest of the game.

Sure enough, Fred came running after the game and stopped in front of me. He handed me one of the pop and sat down on the window sill beside me. The ladies retreated into the store where I was sure they continued their whispering. He talked about the game for a bit and nothing much else that I could remember because my heart was thumping so loud.

I was afraid he could actually hear it! Mom told me that evening Fred had come by but I wasn't home.

That was the evening I went paddling in the canoe and met the bear in the lake. I never knew bears swam that fast. I had just paddled around the bend into the bay when I met the bear. Its eyes looked bug-sore, yet it swam with such speed and determination, and with a "humph!" it veered away from me. He sounded exactly like Hugh, my step-father, though now I just call him Dad and everyone else calls him O. I back-paddled and drifted while I watched the bear reach the shoreline, saw him shake off the water, turn to take a last long look at me, then, disappear into the bushes without a noise. I wished I had some food in the canoe with me. I could have thrown it into the bush where he went in. That sounds just like me. It is only when something is over that I wish I had said or done this or that!

Anyway, back to Freddy... I met Freddy once more after that; quite by accident. I had gone to find a scarf I dropped somewhere along the railroad tracks the day before. I had been out collecting flowers of all sorts the day before, so I went out to retrace my steps. Mom hated the flowers, saying it brought in the bees. But, I liked to have flowers on the table. I knew she was just disappointed that after all her preaching to me about not picking wild flowers since I was a child, it had not done any good. There I was with a handful of wild flowers of all kinds and my scarf threatening to blow away again when I saw Freddy sitting on a rock by the rock-cliff. He just stared at me for a long moment, then he smiled but never said a thing. I continued walking along the railroad until I was parallel to him and stopped. I turned and looked at him and he just sat there smiling. I smiled and then quietly started to laugh. He looked so silly sitting there, totally tongue-tied! Wondering what on earth he was doing there, I was just about to ask when I saw a movement off to the side through the bush. It was a lady with a paddle still in her hand, coming up the path from the portage. It was Karen. She had two small children at home and her husband worked out of town. I saw the look on his face just as I turned and skipped over the railroad tracks, ran around behind the rock-cliff and on to the path that lead directly to Mom's place. My knees were shaking when I came to a stop behind the cabin. She would not have seen me. That was why he didn't do anything. He knew she was coming. He simply had not known what to do! Now, I laughed softly as I got out of the tub. Oh, you never know. Maybe there were other people with her and they had just gone out for a canoe ride. Yeah, and what was he doing there? Why didn't he say anything? I knew back then that I had caught him red-handed. It was that same evening when I got the call from my sister in Nipigon saying that she was working and she wanted me to come and baby-sit for her for the summer.

I got out of the tub and dressed. After lounging around in the room for several hours, I decided to go out for supper. I had to go to the bank to take out some money and I still needed to pick up some food and snacks for the day-long ride to Port Arthur the next day, or rather Thunder Bay as it was now called. I still had to pay a bit more to go to Port Arthur than it would be to get off at the Fort William end of town. Although, I would end up paying more to get a taxi from Fort William to get to Port Arthur... it was cheaper just to pay the extra and get off at Port Arthur. See? It was when I got just like this, that I would drive my mother crazy. "Enough, Channie!" she'd sigh. It had got to a point where I could never carry on a conversation with her anymore. That skinny runt of a step-father always got his measly whiny voice in, cutting me off, as if I had not said anything at all! I yanked on my coat and looked up at the blotch-stained ceiling for a few minutes and took several long deep breaths. I always ended up getting angry about things I could do nothing about. And, since when did Dad become my "step-father" again? Man, he did have a way though of letting you know that you were not wanted!

I came away from the bank with three hundred and sixty dollars in my purse. It was all of my savings from after school jobs and summer program jobs and baby-sitting money. I was feeling care-free and happy as I wandered slowly down the street, looking at the store window displays. Coming back from the grocery store, arms loaded with paper bags, I glanced at the theatre sign. There was a movie there that I might like to see tonight. After depositing the bags on the table in my room, I went slowly back down the stairs, out of the hotel and down the street to a restaurant.

I settled into a corner booth and ordered my supper. Always travelling with a pen and piece of paper, I started writing about what I would do when I got to Port Arthur. I do that before I go somewhere just to see how close or way off I actually will be. I signed my name, Janine, at the top corner of the page before I flipped the page over. That's my proper name. Mother and the older people just called me Channie or Channine. The kids I grew up with just called me Charlie.

Sipping at a cup of coffee, I saw a man get up from the other side of the partition and I knew from the back of his head that it was Fred. He turned and I pretended that I was very busy writing down something important on the piece of paper. Sure enough, I could feel his eyes on me. I heard footsteps and then there he was sliding into the seat across from me.

"When did you come in?" he asked with a broad smile on his face.

He threw his head back to get the left droop of his hair away from his eye. That slow grin seemed to light his eyes into mischievous glints of dark brown pools. I dropped my gaze.

"This afternoon. What are you doing here?"

My paper forgotten, I looked into those dark brown dancing eyes again. I don't know what it was but I always felt that tingle go down to my toes when he looked at me like that.

"I came to get some trapping supplies. Where are you going?"

The waitress came and I ordered and then she was asking if he wanted more coffee. Now he had a cup of coffee in front of him too.

"Port Arthur. When did you get here?"

"Yesterday. How long are you staying?"

He sure made a lot of noise clinking the spoon in his cup as he deposited another teaspoon of sugar. I watched his fingers tightly holding the spoon, stirring and clinking the cup a few more times, as he seemed to be thinking very hard about what he should say next.

"I'm leaving tomorrow. When are you leaving?"

He was putting in some more sugar and rapidly stirring his cup again.

"Can't you stay here tomorrow. Stay another day?"

There went another spoonful of sugar into his cup. I started to smile. How much sugar was that now, five teaspoons? I glanced up into his face and my smile disappeared. He thought I was smiling because I liked what he said!

"We can rent a boat you know. We'll go for a boat ride... and maybe go fishing..."

His face was all lit up and smiling broadly when a lady stood up at the table he had just vacated. Oh my, he was with someone. She turned and gave him a dirty look as she marched down the aisle and stormed out the door. That was bad.

"You left someone sitting there by herself?" I asked, looking over the top of my cup. Steady... my hands were shaking. Keep your eyes down, I thought to myself, concentrate on the cup.

Looking sheepish now, he said, "Just someone I was talking to. She was waiting for her husband actually. He had to go to the bank or something. They have a trap-line."

I knew he was lying to me.

"I am leaving tomorrow," I said.

I watched him take a sip of his coffee and pause before he swallowed very slowly. The waitress came and I smiled and tried to concentrate on the food she placed before me as Fred asked for another cup of coffee. I had to sit there and try to eat with him watching everything I put on my fork, watching it travel to my mouth and watching me very intently as I tried to chew and swallow. I was very hungry but I soon lost my appetite. I was so nervous and uncomfortable with him watching me so closely.

Leaning forward over the table toward me, he asked, "What are you doing after this?"

I had moved until the back seat was pressed flat against my back and now I looked around somewhere else, trying to distract myself.

Any answer I could make would sound like a suggestion or an invitation, so I just said, "Nothing."

"Then, let's go see a movie, eh? Come on, just this once."

That means I would spend the whole evening with him. I felt like running away at the moment. Now what? What was I going to do? The waitress came and put the bill down on the table and Fred had it now in his pocket. This was going too fast, the situation was getting away on me.

I leaned toward him and said, "That is my bill. I'll pay for my food."

He was leaning toward me again, bringing his face very close to mine, looking right at me, he said, "No, I am paying for your meal. My treat. Then I am taking you to the show and we will have a nice evening, alright?"

I leaned back wondering how I was going to get out of this.

Fred was on his feet now saying, "Come on, lets go for a walk."

I stood up and followed him to the counter and watched him pay. Then I followed him out the door and into the street. I felt his hand on my elbow as he started telling me a story about his life in Auden. He led me down the street that led under the railway tracks and on through towards the lake.

He was saying, "One spring, I was cutting wood behind my cabin when these crows started creating such a ruckus over my head. I figured maybe they had a nest close by and wanted me out of there. I just ignored them. Then, the next minute just as I swung my axe to split the wood, one bird dive-bombed me, knocked my hat off and it fell just as the axe blade came down, right on top of it, and I split my hat in half!"

I was laughing hard as he continued.

"And then, there was another time I had a tug-of-war with a seagull. I was fishing down by the lake. I had caught a tiny four inch pike and it had my small jig hook way down its throat and I couldn't reach it with my fingers, so I left it flipping around on the shore and I went up to the cabin to get the pliers. As I was coming back down the path, I saw a big old seagull circling around my fish. Hey! I yelled as I ran down to the lake. Too late, he had swooped down and grabbed the fish. I saw my fishing rod flip around and I dove for it. By now that bugger had swallowed my fish and the fishing line was just singing as I got a good hold of the rod and I started reeling in. He was flapping his wings, getting really ticked off and I just kept turning the handle and he was flapping and flapping his wings, finally he skid landed on the ground and put on his brakes. I kept reeling in and he kept hop skidding closer toward me and finally, his head shot forward and the little fish whizzed by, just missing my face!"

I didn't know whether to believe him or not. His hand on my elbow had slid into my hand and there it firmly held mine. He told me about his wife, his relatives and his aunt. It was evening now and I found myself relaxing at the sight of the lake. I knew his mother had died and he mentioned the relatives he had heard about living all over the place, some he didn't know and others he happened to meet briefly. All he had left that he cared about was his aunt.

I had a fall coat on but the wind was blowing from the north. We stopped by the beach and he stood leaning against a tree.

My voice shook from the cold as I asked, "Do you have any children?"

Quite unexpectedly, he reached and pulled me to him. I felt instant warmth as his arms went around me. He acted like I had always been there and that it was quite natural for him to brush the hair from my face before he brushed my forehead with a kiss. He drew me close once more.

It was a few minutes before his voice close to my ear said, "Not that I know of. My wife was two months pregnant when she was killed. I didn't know about that until they told me after the accident. Nobody else knows. I didn't bother telling the family. I thought I'd only add one more grief."

I stood perfectly still, not knowing what to say. I was in unknown territory, I didn't know how to get out of this situation. I only knew that I wanted out. I wanted to be in control. I didn't like things "happening to me." I wanted to "do" the things that happened. Oh, never mind!

I pushed myself away slowly as I said, "Let's get back, it's getting cold."

He did not object but took my hand firmly again as we retraced our steps back up the street. He wanted to know about my life since we had last seen each other as kids. My story was short, punctured with some funny events in the bush at the trap-line. Nothing was said about the incident by the railroad tracks. It was still half an hour before the show started so, back into the restaurant we went. This time, the conversation was a bit more relaxed. I watched him put one and a half teaspoons of sugar into his coffee. I made no comment about the coffee with the five teaspoons of sugar. An elderly couple beside us caught my attention. The old man was saying in Ojibway, "We'll eat a big meal tonight, we have a long day tomorrow." Freddy was talking about life at home and how difficult it was without any of his family left. When the waitress came, with the old woman being the English speaker, they ordered steak and potatoes. It was when Freddy was into his second cup of coffee that the food came for the old couple. After a while, when Freddy was talking about being at the end of his rope and that he had just up and left his job and that was how he was at the baseball game during the summer... I heard the old woman ask, "Why do they feel they need to put these big green leaves on our plates with the food?" "Oh," said the old man, "they're probably to wipe our hands with." He proceeded to wipe his finger tips with the lettuce.

I smiled, thinking, if there are finger-bowls, then there should be finger-wipe leaves. The only problem was, no one had thought about the "finger-wipe" leaves in restaurants like we use when we eat in the bush.

"What are you smiling at?"

Freddy was looking right at me. Well, I really did not have an excuse why I wasn't listening, so I just said, "I'll tell you when we get out."

A few minutes later, the story actually brought out a loud laugh from him as we headed to the theatre.

There were only a few people in the show. Mainly teenagers up in the front rows. I kept my hands busy with pop and popcorn until about half an hour into the movie when I felt his hand over mine again. He seemed intent in slowly feeling every single one of my fingers. I suddenly jumped as the crashing train in the movie thundered onto the screen and came to a grinding halt right in front of my face. Feeling silly, I turned to Fred and giggled. He was leaning over very close to me and I pushed him back with my elbow as I pulled my hand away and resumed munching on the popcorn. Without being too obvious, my elbow kept him at distance and I kept my hands out of reach by slowly munching on the popcorn throughout the whole movie.

When the movie was over, I knew I had another problem. His arm was still around me as we left the theatre.

"Would you like to stop at the restaurant for a cup of coffee?" he asked.

"Are you kidding, I'm full of pop and popcorn. No, you can go. That's it for me tonight."

I tried to distance myself from his body but his arm was firmly around my shoulder. He made no comment as we made our way to the hotel. As we came through the door, the manager at the desk said, "Hello there, Fred!" I caught the look that passed between them as I went up the stairs with Fred behind me. Darn him anyway! I hated being made to feel like this! I can feel him at my back as I stopped at my door. I waited for him to move away before I would open my door. I finally turned and his hands came up to my arms.

"That's it? You don't want to sit and talk?" he said.

I shook my head. Quite persistently, he continued, "Aren't you going in? Would you like to come into my room for a minute?"

I smiled and shook my head, "No, Fred. It was nice of you to spend the time with me. It was good to talk to you. But, I have to go in now. Take care in the bush. Goodbye."

I turned to unlock the door but he was still standing there behind me. I held the key in my hand and asked, "What are you waiting for? Go."

His hands were now on my shoulders and turning me around when a loud burst of noise came from the bar downstairs. People were coming out and making their way up the stairs.

I moved back quickly and said, "Goodbye, Freddy. Take care." I opened the door and slipped inside just as I heard a woman cry, "Fred, oh Fred! Where have you been? Come here."

I unpacked the groceries and listened to the noise in a room down the hall for a while before I heard them thunder their way back down the stairs. I got my stuff ready to pack in my suitcases and went to bed. The train to Port Arthur would leave before five o'clock in the morning. I thought about the strange evening and soon drifted to sleep.

In what seemed like only a few minutes, I heard some commotion on the stairway and I knew it was Freddy's voice. I looked at my travel clock. After one o'clock! Oh, no! His footsteps are coming to my door. I heard a shuffle against the door and the hesitant knock. Again, a knock. Then I heard him say, "Aw, come on, Charlie. I just want to see you, just for one second. I just need to look at your beautiful face, just one more time... I just thought... please Charlie, keep yourself for me. You are mine you know... remember our parents? They had an agreement, you know, remember? You are mine, Charlie. Don't you ever forget that, okay?"

Another knock. What am I going to do? My heart was pounding. Fear? Yes, I was scared. I was always afraid of drunks! Then suddenly a thought occurred to me that sent a big grin to my face. If you could only hear yourself, Fred! "Charlie, I want you... Charlie, keep yourself for me!"

I silently giggled. Then there was another voice coming up the stairs. It was the woman. Footsteps were coming close to my room, when I heard her say, "Fred, you silly man, that is not your room..." Then I heard a door opening closer by, and the murmur of voices coming from the room across the hall were quite muffled now. They were both inside the room.

Well, you know where you can go, Freddy! What was he talking about... our parents? Yes, I remember hearing something like that. I smiled thinking, keep yourself for me... and what was he doing? Stupid man!

The next morning, with only three hours sleep, I was once again at the station boarding the train to Port Arthur. I found a seat away from the town side and sat with the trees and bushes at my window. I pulled out the sheet of paper that I had written on, on the train to Sioux Lookout the day before. It was to be for today, and I read: "This is going to be a long day, but I look forward to all the stops to see if I know any of the people. I will watch them looking out from their windows and porches. I will wave from my open window or at the doors, knowing how much a wave from the train meant to me when I was the one watching one go by."

I put the paper down and looked out the window. It was beginning to rain outside. I was not going to be waving at people from any open window today.

I sat with my head down. I was very tired. I could feel sorry for myself for awhile. What can I write? I began:

Nothing can penetrate the heavy cloak of loneliness that I am feeling. I had said goodbye to my community yesterday, knowing that I may not be coming back and had not told them about it. The hurt is more intense on leaving Mom, but then I always felt that I had lost Mom when my step-father moved in. What actually hurt more? Losing Mom or leaving Mom? Either way, as long as she was alive and well, she was still Mom whether I was with her or not. The problem here Janine, is that you just don't like your step-father! There, I said it! I hate the measly whiny skinny weasel! I know that I am trying to blame him and the community for my sadness... and trying to shut out the pain I was feeling about Freddy. Now, wait a minute. Why was I feeling bad about Freddy? I am a hopeless romantic that's why! I loved the way he was when we went to the beach. I liked the way he laughed, and I loved the sound of his voice. No. The last voice I heard was the drunken slurred voice at my door. Then there was the suffocating misery and desperation of feeling very much alone, hopeless, and helpless to do anything about anything.

I paused a moment, put my pen down and looked out the window. It was that feeling that had nearly choked me to death the night before. It was a dream that had descended on me nightly... the big black cloud that clamped around my throat and choked me while I struggled for breath, until I discovered a deeper strength from somewhere within me to live. What was this thing? The train was moving now and the conductor was making his rounds. I handed him my ticket and he said a very cheerful,

"Good morning!" I nodded, and looked out the window again, thinking how I hate cheerful people on mornings like this.

I dozed off and on throughout the day, briefly looking around me at each stop and going back to sleep again. It was still raining and what was left of the leaves were blowing around everywhere. I watched the telephone poles march up and down the hills all the way to Lake Superior. The conductor kept stopping by my seat trying to carry on a conversation. I didn't feel like talking. At one stop, an elderly couple got on the train and sat down on the seat opposite me. It appeared that they had been drinking. The old woman was talking about a grandson. Their only grandson, whom it seemed was not much interested in the plans they had for him. Suddenly, the old man focussed his attention on me and asked what my name was, where I came from, and where I was going. That I was not married and never had been, was of quite an interest to them.

Then the old woman leaned close to me and locked her steely black eyes at me and asked quite seriously, "Would you marry our grandson? We have a mine. It is a nickel mine and he is going to be a very rich man. We don't have any other children, you see. We raised him since he was a little boy. Would you marry him?"

If I had ever thought of receiving a proposal for marriage, this was definitely not in my dreams! I just smiled and turned to the window. This was getting really bad and I had a weird sensation in my chest that I was about to burst into uncontrollable laughter. I blinked back tears and looked out the window. To my relief, they got off at the next stop. I never knew what their names were. I picked up a newspaper that someone had left on the empty seat across the aisle from me and I read every section of it. I never knew so many things went on in the world.

It was evening when the slow leisurely ride finally came to an end. The train from Sioux Lookout to Port Arthur had finally reached its destination. I got my snack bag and coat together with my suitcases and stood in line with the few other passengers and descended to the platform amidst blowing wind and rain. I walked with my head down to the waiting room to make some phone calls. There were a few people I could call to see if they could put me up for the night. It was Thursday, so they should be home. Then, suddenly there was Linda grabbing my suitcase on the right.

"What are you doing here?" I said in surprise.

She laughed, "I was waiting for you. Come this way, I parked over there."

I followed her around to the side of the building and there was her little car. We got the suitcases into the trunk and got into the car. It was suddenly quiet inside as the freezing rain pelted against the windshield. She started the car and the heat came on.

"You couldn't have waited long. The air is hot," I said.

Linda laughed as she backed up. "I came tearing down Red River Road trying to beat the train otherwise I'd have to wait to cross the railroad tracks."

I giggled. "Oh yes, I forgot. If you were really waiting for me, how did you know I was coming in?" I asked as we sat at the railway crossing, waiting for the same train to go by.

"Oh, Tom, the mail man called me."

I smiled and said, "And, how did Tom, the mail man know where I was going when I saw him at the train stop yesterday morning?"

Now, Linda laughed outright as the train went slowly by saying, "Your mother was in the store later that morning and told him when he asked, then he called me."

I laughed, "How news travels fast."

Linda lit a cigarette and blew the smoke out the window and said, "I heard all about last night too."

I turned to her as the car sped up the hill. "What about last night?"

She giggled and gave me one of those "side glance lift of the shoulder" things she does when she goes into juicy gossip.

"Well, the guy that works up there saw you with... what's his name? Fred... isn't it?"

I heaved a big sigh and watched the lights go by at Hillcrest Park and down we went and into one of the side streets.

"He said he saw you walking hand in hand to the beach and when he was coming back from his mother's place, he saw you coming out of the theatre with his arm around you and you both went into the hotel."

I leaned over to look at her, "Are you saying this with a straight face or are you eating your cigarette?"

Now, she actually broke into a coughing fit as she pulled into the driveway of her apartment.

"Fred or no Fred, you really should stop smoking those little cigars, you know," I said.

Linda stomped on the cigarette and said, "They are not little cigars, they're cigarettes, they're lighter and not as strong as cigars."

I smiled, "Same difference, they're just shaped a little different that's all."

Now, she was really laughing. "Oh, you really get me each time! We're not talking about cigarettes are we? We're talking about Fred! Oh, clever girl!"

I grabbed the other suitcase and followed her down the four steps to her basement apartment wondering what on earth she meant by that remark, as I watched her bang my suitcase along the sides of the stairs and down against her leg which was tightly encased in purple pants.

CHAPTER 2

Several days later, I got a job at Indian Affairs. Linda worked at the Counselling Unit in Port Arthur and I got a position as a temporary receptionist in the Fort William office. We saw each other at lunch-hour sometimes if she was coming my way, but otherwise we had some pretty interesting suppers together at her place that first month. She brought in take-out food supplemented with my "home-cooked" meals. One time we ended up with egg-rolls and bologna in macaroni and tomato sauce. Another time, we had pizza with fried fish and bannock. One time, we decided to go out for supper and she suggested we order lobsters.

"I don't eat lobster," I said.

"Why?" she asked.

Quite seriously I looked right across the table at her and whispered, "Because they're too much like me... they turn red when they're thrown into hot water."

Linda laughed until she wiped tears from her eyes.

Linda for all her good heart needed some privacy. I had caught her saying on the phone that she couldn't that weekend because she had company. That was it! This was her place and I was in the way so I doubled my efforts to find my own apartment.

At work, I began getting calls from people from my own community who had moved to Thunder Bay and had found out where I worked. They called at all hours of the day and it was beginning to really aggravate my supervisor. As I explained to my supervisor, the first thing a city dweller finds out was that whenever a person from your community knows you are in the city, be assured that they will call on you to help them out. It is expected of them to do so and you are expected to provide the assistance. However, I never got any more calls after the first time each took their turn. I take it I was no help to them whatsoever because I didn't have a car. Now, I'm not saying that I didn't help in other ways.

Some time during the second week, I came home late from work with an arm full of groceries, "greens and fruit" as I called the only fresh things that Linda kept in the refrigerator. Any milk she ever had in the fridge was always rotten or in the process of being, so I, being a non-fresh dairy intake person, being what she called a "natural bush-Indian" couldn't stomach fresh milk, so, the only thing she ever did have in the fridge was the "greens and fruit." She never said she was "going for groceries," it was "going for greens and fruit." Anyway, I had just shut the door with the heel of my high-heeled shoe when I heard her say, "Charlie? Channie? Channine? No, you got the wrong number," and dropped the phone on the hook.

She came into the room, glanced at me and asked, "What's wrong with you?"

"Who was that?"

"I don't know. Same guy, calls once in awhile. Wants to talk to Charlie first and then says Channie or Channine... What?"

"Did you ask him what his name was?"

"Yeah, said his name was Fredrick and he wanted to talk to Channie, Charlie, or something. Why?"

Somewhere deep inside me, a deep rumble of laughter was starting and it slowly travelled up my chest and burst out of my throat before I could take a breath. I was right into a belly laugh when I managed to gasp, "Fred... rick... ! And, he wants to talk to Char... lie... !"

Among the tears of my hysterical laughter, I could tell Linda thought I had surely lost it when she started her hesitant laughter, trying to gauge if she should be laughing at all.

Suddenly, as if she snapped, she turned me around and plopped me down on the kitchen chair and said, "Now, you stop this nonsense, and you tell me who this Fredrick is. Is this the Fred at Sioux Lookout? And who on earth is this Charlie, or Channie, that he's been asking for!"

I crossed my arms over my middle and laughed doubling over until I was able to lean back on the chair. She was now seated across from me with another cigarette going up in quick puffs of smoke. I wiped my eyes and said with a resigned sigh, "Fredrick is the 'Fred' who happened to be in Sioux Lookout while I was on my way down here, and 'Charlie'... well. When we were kids, my family just called me 'Channie' but to the others, I was known as 'Channine' because there is no 'J' sound in the Ojibway language for 'Janine'. It becomes 'Ch' and it soon became shortened to 'Channie' which sounds exactly the same as the Chanii they use for the name 'Charlie'. Chanii is the Ojibway translation of Charlie since there are no 'r' or 'l' sounds in the Ojibway language, they become 'n' sounds in Ojibway. So, I therefore, am Charlie."

A run-away tomato suddenly shot out of the bag and rolled across the kitchen floor and bounced against the potato skin in the corner of the bottom cupboard. I didn't notice the potato skin there before, and now I saw Linda reaching over to pick up the old shrivelled up brown remnant. She didn't touch the tomato but seemed intent on studying the potato peel as if trying to determine how old it was, or how long it had been lying there.

I continued, "Fred has been trying to call me at the office since I got here and I was hoping he wouldn't know where I lived, because I don't want to talk to him. If he calls again, just tell him I don't live here and you don't know where I am, please."

I actually saw her shoulders slump as she shot another puff of smoke into the air and she said, "Well now, how the heck was I supposed to know these things, eh?"

"I'm sorry, Linda. I just didn't want you getting mixed up in this. It felt good to know that I could disappear after work to somewhere in Thunder Bay and he couldn't find me."

Linda smashed her cigarette in the ash tray saying, "Well, now he's found you. So, what are you going to do? Does he know that you don't want to talk to him?"

I felt my body sag against the chair. "I'll find a place of my own and... no, I haven't talked to him yet. Because if I talk to him, I'll never get the chance to tell him that I don't want to talk to him and that I don't want him to call me anymore."

Linda jumped up and threw the potato peel into the garbage, grabbed the bags off the counter and dropped them over by the kitchen sink, saying over her shoulder, "You are not moving away just because you don't want to talk to the guy. If you want me to tell him, I will!"

I saw the tomato gush its guts out under her shoe and she swore as she stood looking at the mess on the floor. I started giggling as I reached to pick up the tomato pulp and then she was there with the cloth to wipe up the mess. Both of us were now squatting on the floor and then she was suddenly facing me, looking at me eye to eye. My eyes dropped to blink back the tears. I finally just threw the tomato over my head and into the sink and settled down on the floor with my back against the cupboard.

Linda flopped down on the floor with her back against the stove and we sat facing each other on the kitchen floor before she said, "Talk."

This was the hardest thing that she always asked me to do. I remember in my second year in high school when she was first assigned to us as our counsellor. It was at a time when I had thought I was near the breaking point. Linda had parked her car on the side of the road and just sat there and waited for me to talk.

"Talk," she said.

It sounded so simple but it was something that I had never done in my whole life! I didn't know how. How could I possibly tell her what I was going through, what I was feeling, what was happening to me? I would sound stupid, ridiculous, self-defeating, self-pitying, whining, confused and totally dumb! And, who would care anyway? What could she possibly do to help me? Nobody cared! I got angry with myself because I started to cry. Finally, I blew my nose, took a big sigh and looked out the window.

She had lit a cigarette, opened her window and said, "Now, talk."

I remember asking, "About what?"

She had replied, "Not 'about what', tell me why? Why do you cry? Why are you feeling the way you do? Why do you not tell anyone what is bothering you? Why don't you tell me, now. Don't worry if it makes any sense or not... just get it all out."

I had laughed at that. And then for the first time in my life, I talked. I talked and talked and talked. When I was finished, I waited for the big "slam down" but got nothing.

I glanced at her and she smiled. She drove to a fast-food take out place and we munched on hamburgers by the park before she asked, "Do you know what you need to do?"

I remember saying, "About what? I can't do anything, what can I do?" No... Yes, but I didn't know until it came out... and then by the time it crashed against my brain, I knew what it was. "Yes, I know now what I need to do."

She had said and continually reminded me over the years that she was there whenever I needed help. I remember feeling emptied out, light, and... clean. Now, here she was again asking me to "talk."

"It's nothing major," I began.

Linda interrupted, "No. No judgements remember? Just talk, straight out."

I smiled at her and said, "Yeah. If I remember correctly, the first time I 'talked' it was like throwing up and cleaning up afterward, and you just sat back and watched."

She smiled at me and sent another cloud of smoke to the ceiling and waited.

I took a deep breath and began, "I don't have a home anymore. I have nowhere to go to, I mean I don't belong anywhere. I feel like I'm trapped when I am at Mom's and I need to escape. I am terrified that one day I may never be able to leave there. So, when I come to the city, I feel such a relief that I can disappear and they can't find me. Because, I like who I am when I am here. I am independent and I want to be on my own. I need to know that I can make it here in the city all by myself. I need to know that I can take care of myself. I think I don't want to talk to Fred because he is very authoritative and I become instantly shy, quiet, and back to the obedient girl that I am... or have to be, when I am back home. I don't want to be reminded of that girl and I don't know if I can be that 'me' in the city and be able to talk to, never mind face, a man who only knows me as the girl back home. Sometimes I have dreams of Fred or somebody like him and I am his wife and suddenly I am like my mother and then the black cloud comes down and tries to choke me to death because... I am not like my mother. When I'm at home it happens night after night—the black cloud, I mean. Or sometimes, I dream that I am at the train station and the train is coming but I can't find my ticket anywhere or I dream that I have absolutely no money at all to get away. I get this horrible cornered feeling, like a caged animal, and I can't get away and that is when this oppressive black cloud comes down and tries to choke me to death and I get so darned scared that I may not wake up again. At times, I actually struggle with both hands at my throat trying to pull or push the black cloud off my neck and face, and I usually wake up just gasping for breath and sweating buckets."

Linda sat there looking at me for a second before she jumped up and made for the table saying, "Gotta have a smoke."

I got up off the floor, rubbing my backside and glanced at Linda as I said, "It's a hard floor for a bony butt."

Linda giggled as she turned around. She walked toward me and slowly put her arms around me and gave me a big hug. I froze. I was not used to being hugged like that. I had never experienced a sister-to-sister hug or mother-to-daughter hug, let alone friend-to-friend hug in my entire life. I didn't know what I was supposed to do! My arms came up and kind of touched dead air between her shoulders. Then my arms dropped. She stood back smiling and I shrugged.

Linda blew another puff of smoke to the darkened ceiling before she said, "I hate it when you do that. The longer you stay here, I'm going to forget to speak altogether."

That, coming from one who's always after me to talk! Let's face it, I had been raised by sisters who had been raised in residential schools, and here I was trying to function as "normal a human being" as I imagined one was to be.

I gave a weak, half-hearted smile at Linda as she gave my shoulders a little pat before we turned to the frying pan on the stove.

"I'll slice up and fry the beef heart I bought and what did you bring, Linda?"

"Chicken chop-suey. Well, that and greens... yuck!"

CHAPTER 3

One day, I came running in during a pouring rain storm to find a tall bald-headed thin man standing in the middle of the kitchen. I stopped dead still by the entrance and started to back out as he said, "Oh, I'm sorry. I startled you. I'm Joe. I'm just waiting for Linda."

Just then, Linda's voice came from the bedroom, "Is that you Janine? Oh, wait a moment... just introduce yourselves."

I closed the door and came in and deposited my wet shopping bag and purse, and peeled off my soaking wet jacket. What a sleazy type, I thought. What does she see in this guy? Oh, well, none of my business. She has never talked about her friends... no need for me to ask.

I went into my bedroom and waited for them to leave with a shout from Linda, "Don't forget to leave the back light on for me."

"Yeah, sure. Have a nice evening!" I stretched myself out full-length on the bed. It was nice to be alone.

The next evening, Linda decided to pick up Joe on the way to dropping me off at the mall. I sat in the car and watched her walk up the few steps to a house on a very busy street. I noticed that the houses were so close to the street that the front steps came out on to the sidewalk. After what seemed like a very long time, they finally came out and Joe was wearing black and red checkered pants. Suddenly, he tripped on the bottom step and shot out full speed into the street with his legs trying to catch up with his head. He was almost to the other side before he got his balance! Four cars went by before he could come back to where Linda stood with her hand over her mouth and I heard her say, "Are you all right?" How he had missed the cars in the heavy traffic, I'll never know! I was near to killing myself laughing before they got to the car. I sat with a straight face when they got in.

When the car finally came to a stop at the mall, I got out and thanked them for the ride and headed toward a bench. There was a big woman sitting there. I sat down beside her and she watched me laugh into my hands.

Between gasps, I managed to say, "I'm sorry, but I just saw something very funny!"

When I finished laughing and sat there drying my eyes, she asked, "So, what was so funny?"

I told her and when I was done, I could see that she did not think it was funny at all. Oh, well, some people have absolutely no sense of humour! I got up and went into the store.

Three weeks later, I got a job interview at the Canada Manpower Centre in Port Arthur as a clerk typist. I remember that interview very well. I had been to the shoe stores the day before trying to find shoes that would match my navy dress, but couldn't find any. My appointment for the interview was at one o'clock sharp and during my lunch-hour, I had ran across the street to a shoe store in a last ditch effort to find a pair of dark navy shoes. Well, after trying on half a dozen navy coloured shoes, none fit, and then next thing you know, it was ten to one. I had only enough time to slip on my old black shoes, run to my office to deposit my coat and then run back across the street to the interview. I came in all out of breath, but on time. I did really well, I thought. I answered all the questions, I was positive, full of spirit, knowledge and enthusiasm. It was only when I got back to the office that I sat back and let out a big sigh.

All the office girls gathered around me to hear how my interview went. Then someone asked how my lunch went with Keith the other day.

Oh, yes, Keith. Keith, the guy who just showed up at the office one day. I sighed. I absolutely loved his sparkling bright blue eyes! His hair was light brown, flowing in gentle waves, and he had the most lovely lips I had ever seen on a man.

"Fine. Well, then at lunch today I went to the last shoe store on the block and tried on at least half a dozen shoes."

I put my feet up on the next chair and noticed in horror that I still had on one of the anklet "try-on-the-shoe-with-these" kind of nylons still draped down around my right ankle! I had gone to the interview with this thing on my foot!

I got a phone call the next day, saying that I had got the job. No one ever said anything about the strange stocking hanging around my right foot.

Soon after that, I found an apartment up on High Street in Port Arthur. It was a nice location, tucked away from the main traffic but close enough to downtown. As the weeks went by, I would walk home and just tilt my head back to smell the fresh air. I knew that I could make it on my own. I had my pay cheque in my purse and I had enough to pay my bills and set aside a bit each month. I always made a point of opening up an account at the nearest bank so I could accumulate enough money that would allow me to leave anytime I wanted to and go anywhere I wanted. Again, this was because of my dread of being stuck in a place that I couldn't get out of without money. For that reason, I always had what I called "get-out money" set aside.

It was around the end of November that it became obvious Keith was really going out of his way with the numerous lunches and quick coffee breaks with me, that yes, he was getting my attention. He had initially started showing up at the office or just calling me on the phone to tell me jokes and, he never failed to make me laugh. He was the only one besides Linda who cared whether I was still alive in this city of strange faces. I wasn't clear about where he worked though. He always wore very nice business suits. All the girls went "ga-ga" every time he showed up. So, I was rather flattered that it was me he was interested in. He'd say something about the insurance business when I tried to press for more information and he'd quickly change the topic.

Took me awhile to figure out how to do this. To be a different kind of human, I mean. But, here I am. I am simply beautiful! Ha, ha, "those lovely blue eyes," eh? Silly girl. I will show you how

31

*lovely I can be, my little lost one! Ha, ha, ha. I am finding this
very weird though, I mean being a white man and all... These
people are deeply set in their ways, where you belong, what you
should say, do, go, and who with. I am finding this very hard to
understand. I also seem to be attracting certain kinds of white
women and I'm not quite sure what to do about that either.*

One evening, Keith called my home number which he got from
Linda. He began calling every evening to tell me which funny movies were
on t.v. Then one night he called to ask if I liked Chinese food. Yes, sure I
did. Anything was better than my cooking at that point. I was even stopping
by at Linda's some evenings on the way home for some of her "bucket of
take-out spaghetti and meatballs." They were fine, but surely not your
everyday meal... but then, neither was my macaroni and bologna! I agreed
to meet Keith at a Chinese restaurant in downtown Fort William.

After over an hour bus ride, I entered the restaurant and paused
at the door. I saw Keith at one of the tables talking to several people
standing beside his table. I took no notice as I walked toward his table, it
was only when I got close that I saw that the man and the two women were
causing him some discomfort and then the blond-haired woman sat down
across from him. It was at this point when I met his panic-stricken eyes. It
was not the man and two women who were causing him this sudden
discomfort, it was me! He didn't want me to be seen by these people. I
turned around and walked back out. I continued down the street, crossed
at the intersection, and stood for exactly three minutes by counting the
usual thousand and one, thousand and two. He was a spineless worm! I
rode the bus all the way home, thinking, "Yes, it was true. He was a
spineless worm. We all know that worms have no spines... or do they? Now,
I am not quite sure about that... I must look that up. Do worms have spines
of some kind?"

The following weekend, he called me saying, "Hi, how are things
going at work?"

"Oh, fine," I answered, then asked, "Aren't you afraid someone's going to find out that you are calling me?"

There was silence at the other end of the line before he said, "Janine, don't get hateful. Please let me come and see you. You have not returned my calls. I'm sorry. I have been driving Linda crazy, calling her everyday because I don't want you to get mad at me. Please, let me explain. It is not what it looked like at the restaurant... please, Janine. Would you like to go to the show with me on Saturday?"

Saturday. I wasn't doing anything on Saturday because I never do anything on Saturday. I hate to sit here again on a Saturday!

I heard myself say, "I will meet you at the nine o'clock show, on Court Street, okay?" Now, why did I say that!

I heard a big sigh of relief and then his voice full of enthusiasm came across the line as he said, "Right on time. I'll see you there. Wait outside, I'll pay your way in. I'll see you then. Good night, Janine..."

I mean, give me a break! Hey, I screwed up. I'm just not used to dealing with these pale-skinned blue-eyed people, they play by their own kind of rules but I'm learning as fast as I can. Actually, I think I'm getting really good at this! I've already learned how to deal with those blond haired women. I just say something like "I'm sorry but I am only interested in having a relationship with my own kind." Ha, ha! The first time I said that, the woman's eyes widened and she walked away without saying a word. Curious reaction. I still fly to my perch on the church steeple when she has gone to bed. I want her. I want her more than I have ever wanted anyone in a very, very, very, long time.

Saturday night came. I had gotten my pay cheque on Friday. I paid my landlord the rent for the next month and I got my groceries for the next two weeks and I put some more money in the bank, and I had a few dollars left. I did not want to be indebted to anybody so I arrived early for the show and paid my own way in. The show was close to starting when I finally decided to line up for pop and popcorn. He still hadn't arrived yet, and I figured that if he came or not, it wouldn't make much difference to me. I just thought that if he came, he could share with me if he didn't mind large unbuttered popcorn and a large Sprite. As I stood in line, I heard a parka-jacket zipper go up behind me and immediately felt the tension on my hair. When I went to move my head, I discovered to my horror that my hair was stuck to the man's jacket zipper stretched full-belching, over his big belly! I twisted to ease the tension as he struggled to push the zipper back down and I ended up with my nose directly against his belly. We were involved in this weird attached dance with our four hands struggling at the zipper and my hair, when the other people around us suddenly swarmed in, laughing and tugging. There were at least half a dozen pair of hands tugging at my hair. One hand hit me against the nose so hard, I thought it was going to bleed! I twisted around again, and then I saw Keith standing there, well away from all the people who were now gathered around us laughing. My head was pressed against the belly of the big man and I actually felt his belly jiggle against my face as he too began to laugh. I did not feel like laughing at all! The more he tried to pull the zipper up the closer my head came up against his chest. There was no way the zipper was going down now. I thought to say something to Keith but the look on his face stopped me. His mouth was hanging open in total horror and he was very ashamed of me. He was even pretending he didn't know me! Then he started to shift to the left and right like a football running-back trying to decide which way to go! A dozen helpful hands were trying to get my hair out now and he just stood there! In blind rage, I yanked my hair as hard as I could and felt it snap one strand at a time as it stretched and broke off against the man's hard metal zipper. With my hair now free in one big wad of tangles at the back of my head, I turned and there was no Keith in sight. I quickly marched out the door and ran down the street and just caught a bus heading toward home.

I entered my apartment, sat down on the bed and burst into tears. I cried like I had never cried before. It seemed the more I tried, the more things went wrong! What could I do? I had tried my best. In fact, what was hurting more was that I knew the problem with Keith had to do with me being an Indian. That was all he seemed to see when we were in public, was the shade of my skin. Or, perhaps he thinks that was what everyone else saw. But, I knew that not all people were like that. I hurt so bad! I was not handling this very well. It just didn't make any sense any way you looked at it! I lay down on the bed and sniffled. I realized I was feeling sorry for myself.

I pulled out a sheet of paper and began writing:

Even getting groceries is getting hard. Last week I was at the counter when I came across one of the racists. I just left the groceries on the counter and walked out. I will never go back there again. Then before that, I was at a shoe store and the manager told me to come back some other time when there was a sale on. I never even got a chance to open my mouth! He clearly didn't want me coming into his store. I remember another time just after that when I had stopped in front of the mall mirrors and looked at myself up and down and I could not see that I looked any different than any other shopper in the store. I had a long summer over-coat on, a dress and high-heeled shoes. And, they all matched. That seemed quite important to me. My hair was neatly styled and my makeup was all in conservative fashion. I thought I looked alright. Then another time, I went into a clothing store and the sales lady came up to me just as I came in and said, "I'm sorry, but we have nothing here for you!" I never got the chance to even open my mouth, so I just turned around and walked out. That's another store that I'll never go back to. You know, at this rate I'm going to run out of stores to shop at.

I put the paper and pencil down on the night table and I slowly started to giggle. I was just trying to make myself feel better about what happened tonight. Keith just wanted to go where there were no other people because he doesn't like to be seen with me alone. Yet, I felt so flattered that he takes an interest in me, mainly because I liked being with him. But, all he seems to be aware of is him in his three-piece business suits and me, no matter how business-like I am dressed, I still have my brown skin and black hair. If only he would get used to the fact that I am an Indian! I found out at the office that as long as I talked and acted like everyone else, they'd soon forget that I was an Indian. I was getting very good at acting, talking, reacting, and communicating just like them, that I was beginning to be just like them. I just wanted to fit in somewhere where I didn't always stick out. I rolled myself into a ball inside my quilt and fell asleep.

Alright! I am not very good at being a white man. How on earth is a person supposed to know what to do? When I showed up during the hair and zipper scene, there right behind her was the business man who had introduced me to his daughter. I had to tell that woman too that I was only interested in my own kind. She too was aghast and quickly retreated. Hmm, very curious reaction. Very powerful words. I must figure out something else... Oh, before I fly away, I must say that these city ravens are very nasty and aggressive creatures! When I first arrived and settled on top that church steeple, Big Kaa came after me. How was I supposed to know that was his territory. He tormented me for so long, I finally got fed up. I clamped my beak on that old raven's wing and pulled him down to the ground where I became a wolf and I had him for lunch! Ha, ha, ha...

CHAPTER 4

The next morning Fred awoke to a splitting headache and Gladys' voice coming from the bedroom, "Hey, Fredrick. What's taking you so long? I'm waiting for you, you know?"

He leaned over the bathroom sink and looked at himself in the mirror. He needed a shave, rather badly. He hated this. He hated the morning after when there was a woman in the bed waiting for him. He grinned now at his reflection, thinking, I'm useless when I drink, so they wait until the next morning, at which time, I want nothing to do with them... then they throw things at me or call me all kinds of obscene names.

He looked at his crooked grin in the mirror. Just wait until he told Gladys that he would have to ask for another I.O.U.

Oh, Charlie!, he thought, I wish you were ready, but you are not!

"Fredrick!"

He entered the bedroom and sank down at the foot of the bed with his head in his hands and moaned, "Sorry, Gladys. I can't seem to get this drinking and hang-over stuff right."

He heard her give a big sigh behind him as she kicked the blankets off the bed and jumped up and stood naked in front of him. Then slowly, she began to get dressed. But, all he thought of was Janine. This is really crazy, he thought! He knew that Gladys would not complain to anyone else because she would sound like she wasn't worth much if she couldn't even keep him, of all people, satisfied. He smiled. This business worked both ways.

He had had no idea that Janine was still in the community that night. Her sister had told him the week before that Janine was already in Port Arthur. He wondered if she had deliberately lied to him. But, why? He crawled into bed and lay face down on the bed.

Eventually, he heard Gladys leaving the room and as usual, she made sure that she banged the door behind her. He smiled and turned over to his back. Well, Charlie was now in Thunder Bay. He had watched her since she was a child. His mother had told him that Janine's father had a debt to his own father for saving Janine's father's life when he had fallen through the ice with his dog team and he had promised his daughter to the other's son when she was no more than three years old. The men had no doubt as to their children's future, but then they had both died. That left his mother and Janine's mother. Then his mother had died next and that left just Janine's mother who knew of the arrangement. He thought that she chose to ignore it and maybe she had not even told Janine about the arrangement. Well, one way or another, she would be his. She had always been and always would be his. Whether she acknowledged it or not, she would be his. What bothered him now was that she no longer had a father to make sure that she was not touched by any other man other than himself. That left no one but him. Now, how was he supposed to do that without spying on her? He looked at the mottled ceiling of the hotel room thinking, I know I should not have married Mary. I had married another girl when I was already spiritually married to another who was to have eventually become my real wife. I had done wrong. The Elders who approached me at the funeral that time told me so. Now, just yesterday, there I was facing the girl and I had no way to reach her. She would never have understood me.

He had tried once to tell Janine about their future together, but she was too young and she had not understood. He had also been drunk when he had gone to the cabin demanding that her mother open the door. She had. Janine was only thirteen years old then and she looked so beautiful, fast asleep in the back room. He had bent over her for a good two minutes before he touched her face, then she had sprung to life, cursed him, screamed at him and hit him, and literally kicked him out of the cabin!

Grinning now, he remembered that he had picked himself out of the snowbank in front of her doorstep and walked home quite assured that if he couldn't get near his future wife, then no one else could either!

After seeing her lately though, he wanted her like he had wanted no other woman before. He was also beset with a fear that she would somehow find another man before him and... well, the deal would be off then. That was what he did not want. He wanted her and only her! And, he wanted her now. "Oh, Charlie, please don't forget me!"

He fell into a deep sleep. In his dream, she was with him. She was with him and she would be his but he would have to work hard. He saw her with an outfit more appropriate for the city and she stood in the middle of his trapper's shack at Clay Lake. He had felt embarrassed and sad that he could not provide her a better place. What hurt more was that she had looked so out of place. She deserved something better, to be somewhere better, better than what he would ever have to offer!

He awoke with such a start sometime later in the evening in the Sioux Lookout Hotel room. It was only a few minutes before the evening train came that would take him back home. He decided to scramble and make it to the train station on time. He would go to the trap-line and get things ready for her.

He got on the train that night determined that he would focus on her and nothing else would side-track him in the coming months. He would convince her to stay with him when all his plans were completed.

He got off the train and immediately his eyes swept over the crowd searching for Karen. "Out of habit," he thought as he picked up his boxes and walked to his cabin, determined that he was going to be alone this night. He must make an effort to stay away from Karen so he hurried away toward his cabin as quick as he could. He unlocked the door and entered the cold dark room. He hated coming home to this; into a cold and dark home. Sometimes out at the trap-line, he imagined coming home to a nice warm cabin, with the lamp light falling on Janine's smiling face and the room filled with the smell of a good hot meal. He lit the coal-oil lamp and soon got the fire going. He didn't want to stay here, so he went next door to visit Sheila and Bob. He was sure to get a good hot meal there while he poured out drinks from the bottle of whiskey in his jacket pocket.

After several nights of partying and the nights spent with Karen, he finally got around to making arrangements and got ready to leave for the trap-line. He got Sheila and Bob to set up his old family cabin for Janine. He promised them both that he would bring his long-awaited wife home for Christmas. When he got to the trap-line he arranged the cabin as much as he could. He brought a vinyl kitchen table cloth with red and pink flowers and draped it over the old wooden table. Next he covered the exposed wooden shelves along the walls. He brought sleeping bags with flowery designs which he threw over the double bed, along with two extra pillows. Finally he hauled pails, frying pans, bowls, dishes and cups from his house at the community on the last trip.

Around the first week of Christmas, he got distracted by Karen again with her endless stashed bottles of rum or gin. She demanded nothing, asked for nothing, and only gave a bit of happiness for a few hours, before she disappeared into her cabin again. She had a certain dignity and maintained her position as the community "stay-at-home-wife" to take care of the kids while her husband was working in Winnipeg. When she had to get some wood, her neighbour came to look after the kids. She joked and laughed, perhaps her only chance to laugh after several weeks. We all did what we could to survive. She was there for him and he had always been there when she needed him. But, Janine, now... well, that could cause some complications. He had waited a long time but his time would come. He just had to make sure that all the things were there that she would need.

He had called several times to Indian Affairs and the Canada Manpower Centre, and then one day he got the number to Linda's place from his old friend, the postmaster. Still there had been no answer until Linda picked up the phone. He knew then that he had the right house. Now, if only Charlie would pick up the phone! She never did. He could not afford to lose touch with her now.

In the second week of December, the cabin was all set and he had brought all the supplies for her, but he never got through to her on the phone. He went back to the trap-line and worked hard at trying to accumulate enough pelts for him to come out again and to try to call her.

He would remove all his traps, estimating the length of time he expected to be gone. When he got back to the community, he was on the phone again.

He had tried calling her many times. She never answered until that one evening a week before Christmas when he was ready to go back to the trap-line without her.

Chapter 5

I did not answer any more phone calls at home for the next few days it took to get my number changed, until that night on the week of Christmas. I had been feeling rather poorly, whether through a cold, depression, or loneliness, I cared not which. I wanted to go home so bad. Christmas was nearing and I still could not find a reason to go home at all. I had arranged a signal for Linda's calls. I would know it was her if she let it ring once, followed by three more rings. I would then pick up the phone on the fourth ring.

It was on one of these rings that I picked up the phone and said, "Yeah, Lin. Why don't you go home to see your mother? Why are you here calling me?"

There was silence at the other end of the line for a few seconds before I heard a voice say, "Charlie. I'm coming to get you. Get your bags packed. You are coming home with me. I need you with me this Christmas... please Charlie."

It was Freddy! His soft voice triggered something in me.

I took a deep breath and then gathering up my courage, I quickly said, "I... I could see you in Armstrong on the 20th. Do you think you could be there around seven in the evening? I'll try to catch a ride with the last batch of students going home."

Freddie's voice came back saying, "I can't wait to see you again. Take care of yourself... and please keep yourself for me."

He always says that! What on earth does he mean by that?

I arrived in Armstrong in a van with some students and had just waved goodbye to them as they boarded the train, when I felt a pair of arms come around my waist. I turned and there was Freddy. I had never been so happy to see anyone! Never had I needed so much love and support as I did just then. After a slow meal and a lot of conversation in the restaurant, I actually welcomed the way he always took control of the situation. And, without hesitation, I allowed him to lead me to his room at the hotel and he made me feel like the most loved person in the whole world.

The next morning, I looked at the glistening frosty window and knew that all I had needed was someone to love... and then, there was no mistaking at that moment, I wanted to go back to the safety of the city. I had been a virgin. I was no longer. For some reason, I felt quite empty inside.

I watched Fred roll over on to his back and he whispered beneath his breath, "Charlie, what are you doing standing there? You are shivering from cold. Come here. I will keep you warm. I will always keep you warm."

I slowly slipped back in beneath the blankets and instantly felt the warmth of his legs and arms as they enveloped me. I looked long and deep into his dark brown eyes. They were filled with wonder and perhaps a bit of disbelief, but open and loving. I slowly brushed his hair away from his forehead, thinking that since I was a little girl, I had looked close at him but had never touched him. Now, I traced my finger down his nose, to feel his lips kiss my finger, then down over his chin, I trailed my finger to his throat. I felt his face, down his arms, his legs, and along his whole body. I adopted his body as part of my own and he became a part of me. Never again, would I feel alone.

We decided to go home to the community on the evening train with all his boxes of groceries and trapping supplies. It was now December 21st, and we were still debating whether to head out right away the next morning and spend Christmas all by ourselves in the bush at his cabin or whether to hang around until all the community had celebrated the holiday. I was all for getting away as soon as possible to the bush.

I hated to face my mother and step-father. I could just imagine what they would have to say about Fred. My step-father had no use for him. There were some comments that I remembered he had made about Fred and his then new wife that I had never understood and never cared to listen

43

to. And then there were the others. How would they feel about his taking me as his wife? What about the other women in the community that he'd been with? I couldn't forget that. How could I look them all in the face and say that I knew what I was doing? To be honest, if and when I faced them, would I have the nerve to tell them that it was he, Fred, that I had picked to be my husband? My husband? The thought brought heat to my cheeks and an ache of fear in my belly. I knew right then that I couldn't do it!

We were now at the train station waiting for the train. I had already come across some people from the community and the reaction had not been very good when they saw that I was with Fred. I looked at him standing there, tall and proud. He always had a half smile on his face as if all the world was a pleasure for him to behold each and every day. I liked the way he stood with always one knee bent when he spoke to someone. I liked the way that one lock of hair always curled up over his left ear whereas the right side curled and tucked neatly underneath. There were things about him that I was picking out as a personal acknowledgment that he was mine. He was my husband to be. When I looked at him when we were alone, I saw life as a happy future but then things quickly got jumbled up when other people came into the scene. At those times, I was suddenly not quite sure about anything. Right now, I had only thought so far as the holidays. Yes, I would go and spend Christmas at his trap-line and then head back to the safety of the city after the holidays.

My problem right now was that I was not comfortable being with him when we met the people from the community who were also on their way home from a day of shopping. I felt like the women knew what I had just found out and I also did not like the feeling I got when Fred deliberately put his arms around me in public. It was like he was showing off his most recent acquisition. They looked at me like I did something wrong and that they were deeply disappointed in me.

Right after we boarded the train and gave our tickets to the conductor, Fred just got up and left the seat beside me. I never saw him again until the train was coming to a stop at home when he appeared behind me, breath smelling of liquor. My anxiety increased right after we got off the train. Fred insisted I follow him to the man's cabin that he had been drinking with on the train and when I didn't want to, he literally pushed me ahead of him.

As we neared the place, I could see from the shadows of the windows and the noise coming from the cabin that there was a party going on. I turned to say that I should perhaps see what was happening at Mom's, when Fred firmly nudged me from behind signalling that I was not to turn around. When he pushed me through the doors. I dropped my suitcases to the side and stopped. Fred took a firm hold of my arm and dragged me around past the table and into the side room and toward the other room while I was being pulled from every direction by people sitting on every chair and space available.

All the while, I listened to Fred exclaiming, "Yeah, see! I went and got her and dragged her home! She is mine! Look! Isn't she beautiful? She's been getting more and more beautiful every year and now she's mine. She is going to be my wife! Eh, Charlie? You're all mine!"

I had such an ache in my stomach that I literally felt like throwing up. I was pushed forward again around to everyone in the room that when I finally ended up where my suitcases still stood, I twisted around and went into the porch, closed the door and grabbed my suitcases. I was out the door and down the railroad tracks in five minutes flat! I practically ran all the way along the uneven snow-trodden path along the railroad tracks toward the swamp.

Finally, I cleared the creek and ran all the way up the hill. I paused a moment to catch my breath. Then I looked behind me to see the black and white dog. The silly dog was coming up to me wagging his tail. I set my suitcases down on the snow on each side of my feet. Here I was again at my rest stop. I heard nothing besides the dog's tail brushing the snow. There was only the sound of my hard breathing, the loud thumping of my heart... and then the tears came.

My stupid girl, what have you done? I was with you all the time and you always act like you don't see me. When you do see me, you don't recognize me! Her tear just landed on my nose and I taste the salt of it. Her arm pulls me closer to her. I feel her pain. My poor lost one. If she only knew what I had just arranged for her new fiancé. He'll pay for this. I will punish him. He has taken my beloved and caused her pain... pain... pain.

I let the tears stream over my face until I became afraid of getting frost-bite on my cheeks. What was happening to me? I did not like what was happening to me! Where was Fred? Why did Fred act like he did with those people? Or maybe I should ask, why was Fred the way he was with those people? It was like he became different. He was not the Fred I knew in private... he was like a different person in front of those people.

The moon was shining bright and it was a cool crispy night of December 23rd. I couldn't believe how much I had gone through in just two days! I picked up my two suitcases and continued down the path. I could see a light at my mother's cabin. They must still be up. The dog followed me as the snow crunched unusually loud under my feet. As I approached the cabin the dog next door started barking. I stepped on the porch and pushed at the door. It was locked. I pounded on the door and there was no sound.

I pounded on the door with my fist once more and called, "Mother, it's me, Channie. Open the door."

Still, there was no sound. I put my suitcases down and stepped back. A light was on inside. I could tell by the light that it was the coal-oil lamp that was on. And, I could tell by the smoke from the stove pipe that someone had recently put fresh wood in the stove. I approached the door once more. It was then I noticed that there was a stick of wood over the padlock loops on the door. I pulled out the stick and pushed the door open and walked in. The light was bright against my eyes.

I stood a moment before I slowly walked to the back of the room. There was no one in the front room where the coal-oil lamp stood at the table beside the double bed. I walked forward to check the back room where there was another double bed in one corner and several dressers flanked by another single bed by the back window. That's the bed I used to sleep on. Now I was standing at the doorway letting my eyes adjust and trying to collect my thoughts. There was no one in the cabin. I went and got my suitcases, put them on the single bed, turned up the light, and threw more wood in the fire.

The two little squirrel-brained Groundhogs should be making their appearance now, I supposed. They usually did, since it was now way past the last train. The Groundhogs were my step-father's twin sons from his first marriage. They were now around twelve or thirteen years old. They were here to stay. Good arrangement for his ex-wife, I'd say. Why didn't the boys see me getting off the train? They probably weren't there, which means they were probably going to the place I had already been since I got off the train. I boiled some water, made some tea and waited. It was exactly twenty after twelve when Benny and Lenny came crashing through the door.

"Janine! Oh, man, Charlie! We're so glad to see you! Oh, man! You wouldn't believe what happened when Fred told Dad you were his wife and then there was no you, and then Fred had to prove that there was a 'you' before we came in and then your Mom said that you probably had gone home since Fred hadn't given you a home yet, seeing as he didn't have his own home to give you, then Fred said that you definitely were his Mrs. Fred to be... and, well... that was, well... when she punched him full in the mouth!"

I looked at the solid, thick brown-haired and chubby rosy-cheeked face in front of me. Was it Benny or Lenny? I felt the cup slip from my hand and quite detached, I watched the cup hit the floor in slow motion as I said, "Mother... hit Fred in the mouth?"

One of the twins picked up the cup—don't know which one—and then he was in front of me saying, "Oh, yeah, even Dad was really peeved off that you would choose Fred of all people!"

The other one of the nymphs piped up saying, "Yeah, even Mam was really beefed that you would pick Fred! Aww, come on Charlie, you are the most beautiful girl in this place and all around, everybody says so, and you are really smart... even Mam says so! Ah, come on, now... don't cry."

I said, "Just go away from me a minute."

I got the mop to dry the tea off the floor. They never say things like that to me! No one ever told me I was smart! They never told me I was someone they cared about! It is only when we do something wrong, or when it is too late, always too late to undo things that they tell us they cared. Well, it's too late for me! Why didn't they tell me before I did this! It may have made a difference... maybe... but then, maybe not. Fred would have found me one way or another.

I kicked off my boots, cleared off my suitcases and rolled up on top the single bed. It was some time later that I felt someone put a warm blanket over me. I listened to the boys chatter for a good half hour more before I heard them crawl into their double bed in what used to be my room. They had just arrived last spring. Their mother didn't want to look after them anymore, I heard. I didn't think I would be able to sleep. I listened to every squeak of the logs and the snap of the oil-lamp that was again turned down low.

It was around seven o'clock in the morning when my mother and step-father came through the door. I sat bolt-upright wide awake as they stomped in arguing about finding the perfect mate for Warts, then I promptly dropped my head back on the pillow and rolled over. A mate for Warts, the dog, was the least of my worries!

CHAPTER 6

Fred walked along the path with the snow crunching under his feet. It had been an awful night! He thought back to a few nights ago when he had called Janine in Thunder Bay. He had just been totally taken by surprise when she had suggested that he meet her in Armstrong! She had come to him willingly like someone who knew to whom she belonged. She was his and he became hers. With heartfelt thanks, he had discovered that he was the first with her. She was his. He whispered a silent message to the early morning sky, saying, "You had looked after her grandpa, you had saved her for me. Now, help me make her mine forever!"

It was only yesterday morning that reality hit him when he saw her standing at the hotel window. Oh, she had looked so beautiful. Like an angel out of a story book, she had stood against the early morning sun and her form was perfect against the light. Her hair hung in heavy dark waves down her back. She always seemed totally unaware of her beauty during the course of the day. He wondered if she was ever aware or had ever realized that people were generally extra kind to her. He thought that maybe if there was a problem with her, it was just that. From the time that he could remember first seeing her, when she was just a little girl, she had taken all things for granted. She did not know people didn't usually act that way with other people as they did with her. Yet she seemed to always expect this treatment and surprisingly, she always got it! How did that happen? He didn't know anybody else who could do what she did to other people! He had seen her shiver in that cool hotel room. It occurred to him that it was an awful place to have made her, his. But, soon she had been snug and warm in his arms again. How was he going to keep her there? When she found out that he just lived a totally humble existence, what was going to keep her to him? He couldn't expect her to love him as much as he loved her. No. Nobody could do that.

The next morning as they waited for the train at the train station, he had seen Old Henry of all people. There was Old Henry at the station platform giving him a dirty look.

Old Henry had walked up to him last month at the store in the village, bold as he pleased and said to him for all to hear, "Don't touch that girl. You're no good for her anymore! You know what you're called, son? You are a broken person! Let the girl go, leave her alone! If your father was alive, he would tell you the same thing that I am telling you now!"

He had been so infuriated that he had just looked at the old man and decided that here was one life that would not last very long if he had anything to do with it! On the train, the old man had sat down behind them and that was when Fred decided that he was going to be elsewhere for the length of the train ride. He had left Janine and went to the Club Car. There he saw some drinking buddies from Sioux Lookout who immediately pressed drinks into his hand. One was indebted to him for help in the majority of his house repair at Allanwater Bridge and the other had a very nice deck addition to his home in Sioux Lookout that Fred had managed over a weekend last summer.

Fred loved helping people. There wasn't a thing he would not do for others. He was always full of joy and genuinely forth-coming in his offer of assistance, and he was well known to have a tremendous ability to help people in all situations. He prided himself in the knowledge that he could do anything he put his mind to. He never asked for money or anything other than that he would expect assistance in return, should he ever need it. People took him up on that offer, and to date, he had never asked anyone for anything. In some places, the people said, "If you need help, call Fred. He'll know what to do. He'll help you." So, right about that time, he did not want to see Old Henry. He remained in the Club Car until the conductor came by to announce the next stop.

He was determined that he was going to introduce her to everyone. They must all know that she was his. This was his one night to stake his claim on her for all to see for themselves! It did not quite end up like that. After pulling her through the mob in the front room, he was heading for the guys when he was pulled aside by Karen. Oh, she had a way of side-railing him! She did it on purpose, he knew. But the intrigue and play in public always fascinated him and before he realized it, Janine was no longer behind him. Well, what was he to do? With perfect timing Karen disappeared when Janine's mother and step-father materialized in front of him just as he was in the process of saying that Janine would be married to him by spring. He had felt the push and a sting to his lips before he realized that Janine's mother had hit him! He had reeled back and stepped out of the room on the pretext of helping old Josephine out the door with her canes.

He had walked the old woman to her cabin and had then ran to Karen's place. That wench! That wasn't the first time she had deliberately gotten him into trouble! She was an expert at manipulating circumstances to give them time together before her husband was home. She held the door open for him when he arrived, brushing a kiss across his cheek as he went into her bedroom. She had been patiently waiting. He had taken a bit longer than she had expected. Well, it was old Josephine to blame for that, he had said, "go ask her."

Now he was approaching Janine's parent's cabin. What would she say? Would they let him in? He took a deep breath and knocked on the door.

CHAPTER 7

I opened my eyes to find Benny, or was it Lenny, at my bedside smoothing the hair off my forehead just as the pounding sounded at the door. He was gone, and then Warts, the dog, started barking next door. I heard my step-father, or O as everyone called him, opening the door and then I heard Freddy's voice. My heart bumped against my throat. Oh, what a complete turn-around double-faced... he was bringing bacon and eggs! I actually heard him insisting on making the coffee and frying the eggs while he waited for Mother to get herself on her feet. I could imagine him watching Mother getting up off her bed beside the kitchen table and coming into our shaded-off area to dress.

That was where I caught her with my insistent whispering, "What on earth are you doing?"

"What do you mean, what I'm doing?" she whispered back.

"Why is he here?" I asked, perhaps too innocently, because I flinched as I too changed my clothes quickly.

"He is here to get the rest of you. By that, I take it he already got the first of you so now he's here for the rest of you. If that is not true then you had better speak up. Otherwise, why is he here? You tell me that!"

I had no answer. It was almost nine o'clock, the train would be here soon. I had to get out! I was getting that suffocating feeling in me again! I threw my dirty clothes back into the suitcase and grabbed my jacket and put my boots on. Mother watched me but said not a word as I picked up my suitcases and walked out of the bedroom and into the kitchen.

Fred was at the table with his back to me and I took a close look at him and somehow, for a moment, it was as if I didn't know him at all!

I started to panic deep inside and then he turned around and levelled those dark brown eyes into mine and he said, "Charlie, please, don't disappear like that on me again." He was off the chair and coming toward me saying, "I love you, Charlie, I need you Janine."

Then, he was in front of me and his arms closed around me tightly. My suitcases kept my arms straight and pressed against my legs but I refused to let them go. I have to be strong! I stood there not moving. Then he moved his face back to look at me. He smelled of stale liquor and where did he spend the night? I had given him something pure and unused and he was giving me an old filthy used rag in return! I pushed hard and he staggered back and then I was out the door.

I did not pause but kept my feet moving one after another. I was up by the hill when I heard him calling me. I heard his footsteps catching up behind me. I kept at a constant pace. Soon, he was behind me and he clamped his hands on my shoulders just as I was crossing the little bridge over the creek.

He stood there panting, "Why? Charlie, you can't leave like this! Please, come to the bush with me. Remember we had planned to leave today? What are you doing?"

I turned and looked up at him saying, "Why didn't you remember that last night Freddy? Where were you last night Freddy? What did you do last night Freddy? How can you stand there and ask me, why?"

I whirled around and continued walking, thinking, as each step hit the soft snow that had fallen sometime during the night, this is stupid, this is stupid, we are having a fight and we don't even have enough of a commitment to each other to have anything to fight about!

Suddenly, I stopped dead still in my tracks as a thought hit me with such force that I felt a shock go through me from head to foot—what if I had gotten pregnant!

He was so close behind me, perhaps to say something else that when I suddenly stopped, I felt his teeth hit the back of my head so hard that I momentarily forgot my shock as he exclaimed, "Gull darn it! Why the heck did you stop so suddenly for? Oh, god!"

I looked back to see him leaning over spitting in the snow. There was no blood. He said, "Come here. I'll check to see if your head is bleeding." He stepped closer behind me. "Your head's okay."

I turned and looked up at his face for a moment, noticing that the curls along his temples were sticking up in between the hanging strands of dark hair. Then he put his head down with such a dejected look, I touched the top of his head. It was then that I started laughing. Like a dam suddenly breaking, I was leaning over laughing, laughing as hard as I could. It was then that I heard him begin to laugh hesitantly before he looked at me. Wiping the tears from my eyes, I saw him standing there knowing that he knew that I knew something had come to an end before it had even begun.

I picked up my suitcases again and started to walk away. Still, he had not moved. I didn't want to leave him standing there, so I turned and sounding almost a bit too chippy or merry, I said, "Go! Have a good time... have a good holiday. Take care of yourself... and Merry Christmas and all that." I smiled.

He did not answer. I turned and hurried down the path because I could hear the train coming now. The black and white dog joined me at the makeshift station as he ran from the store with the mail clerk. After a quick lick at my hand, I stopped to run my hand to the top of his head. Such a nice dog! I boarded the train without a backward glance.

Ah, my poor lost little one, a grand warrior will soon come to rescue you from that insufferable losing cheat!

Back in Thunder Bay, I opened my apartment door and went in. It was around ten o'clock at night when I hit the light switch and entered the kitchen with my suitcases. I stopped and looked around at the bare walls. The clean bare counter, the bare kitchen table and the bare... everything. The rented furnished apartment that it was, was exactly what it looked like. I decided that I was going to have a shower, get cleaned up and go to bed. I decided to go shopping early the next morning for Christmas decorations, perhaps a little fake tree, decorations and some supper treats. Yes, and I would have a lovely Christmas all by myself!

I had just finished unpacking and was getting ready for the long hot shower when the telephone rang. After the initial heart jump, I soon recognized Linda's ring and I quickly picked up the phone and heard her voice saying, "Oh, Janine. I'm so glad you answered the phone. I called last night about this time but there was no answer. I called again around half past eleven too, and there was still no answer. I just wanted to know if you were there or if you had gone home... so, you are still there?"

I heaved a big sigh of relief and said, "Yeah, I'm still here. Who did you think you were talking to? My ghost? No, I'm sorry I said that. You must know I'm home or would be coming home, otherwise you wouldn't call. I'm doing fine and I've decided to go downtown and do some shopping tomorrow, or maybe do some visiting... or whatever. So, you're at your mother's place?"

Her voice came back on the line saying, "Yes, I'm at her place in Hamilton and I'm sorry if I made a mistake in giving your home number to Fred, but I just thought that since he was from your community, you would be safer with him or... what I mean is, that you would have a better idea what to expect from him... or that you'd have a good Christmas. Anyway, I'm glad you're home and I know that you're safe, have a great holiday and I'll call you back when I get home."

I answered with as much enthusiasm as I could muster, "Yes. Happy Christmas wishes to your mother. Have a great Christmas... and listen, I may not be here, in fact, I may be leaving tomorrow, so don't call back until after the holidays, okay? And, don't worry about me! Have fun, bye."

After a quick shower, I lay in bed flat on my back with my hands to my sides. What would it feel like to be dead? I wonder what I'd look like if I was dead and lying here like this. No, I think they have the hands crossed like this. I suddenly started to giggle, this was ridiculous! I don't know what got me thinking about that. I turned to my recent acquisition in the corner of my bedroom. It was a twelve-inch black and white television. It only had two channels but I at least got the local news or some odd show or old movie once in awhile. I rubbed my tummy as I felt another cramp. Almost every waking hour since that one thought occurred to me at the time Freddy nearly embedded his front teeth in the back of my scalp, I had been riddled with a guilty conscience and anxiety. What if I had gotten pregnant! I did not want a baby and I swore to and vowed to everything I could think of that could possibly aid in preventing such a thing from happening.

It was with immense relief when I discovered that my menstruation was right on time the next morning. I hummed our childhood version of Dashing Through the Snow. As near as I could translate, our Ojibway version went something like this, "Dassing peenda moo." Which, by the way, was "there is poo in my pants" in the English translation, followed by all the jollifications that follows over the fields being in that condition. Hmph!

I headed out for downtown amidst outside side-walk intercom Christmas carols. I loaded up on decorations and some yarn to knit and make myself a homey place to live. I came back rather tired after a whole day of bus rides and three shopping malls, and nothing left of my spending money for the month.

My knitting and crocheting alternated between Christmas decorations, and picture frames, along with my many songs of thankfulness and promises never to do such a thing again! But at night in my bed, Freddy was there in my mind. I imagined the sound of his voice. I visualized the way he walked and talked. I loved his gentleness with me. It would have been nice to be with him. But, when morning came, I loved my freedom. I loved my independence. Yes, I loved being on my own to do what I liked, whenever I liked.

Then on New Year's Eve, the phone rang. I was watching a comedy on the local channel when I grabbed the phone.

"Hello."

"Hi, Jan. What are you doing tonight?" It was Keith and he sounded very down.

"Keith? Well, I'm not doing anything actually. I've got my feet up, I have a pillow at my back and under my elbows, a bowl of chips and dip, and I'm just watching a comedy on t.v. This guy is trying to juggle bowling balls, you should try that sometime. Why do you ask? What are you doing?"

I heard him heave a big sigh as he said, "Nothing. I am doing nothing at all. I thought maybe, you'd want to go to the show with me?"

I slowly dropped the phone back onto the hook. I don't know why I talked to him at all. I watched a person swing his arms totally around and proceeded to turn his body from back-side to front on the television. Oh, well, the world was full of strange people. I shut the television off and curled up in my warm blankets. Tomorrow was a brand new year. I wasn't looking forward to another year like this one. I took out my notebook and started writing about how I would like the next year to be. I imagined a cabin by the lake close to the city and someone. No, I'll just concentrate on me. But, Fred kept interrupting my thoughts and I had nowhere to fit him in my dreamland. He seemed so out of place there. I put my book away and shut off the light.

Well, this white man thing is not working. So, I will be her handsome dashing Anishinabe who will be so undeniably wonderful and supporting and I will make her love me and be my own wife!

On New Year's Day, around supper-time, I had just pulled a roast out of the oven when there was a knock at my door. My heart thudded against my chest as I looked at the door. No one knew where I lived. Who could that be? I walked to the door and looked out the window. There was a Native man standing there with his head down. Thoroughly puzzled, I opened the door and asked what he wanted.

He said, "I am so sorry to bother you. My name is Nisha, from your community. My truck, there at the corner, broke down and I happen to glance at the street sign and I remembered your address. You see, I was the one who put the address on the envelope for your mother when she sent you the letter."

I nodded. I knew who he was. I remember people talking about him in the community. Just showed up one day. He comes and goes. Never actually said who he was or where he was from. Helps people out, stays awhile and then he's gone again. Heaven knows how long before he shows up again. From what I hear, he's quite reclusive, I mean, doesn't answer personal questions, but somehow it just doesn't seem to matter once you start talking to him.

He continued, "I just wanted to know if I could use your phone. I need to call a tow-truck or something."

I stood aside for him to enter. He glanced at me and then stepped in. I showed him the phone and went back to the kitchen and became busy by the stove. I heard him talking on the phone and then he came in and sat down at the kitchen table.

I was taking out the yams from the oven when he said, "I was trying to decide what smells so good. Ham, potatoes, carrots... right?"

I took two cups down saying, "Do you take your coffee black? Or with cream and sugar?"

"Yes, any way. Doesn't really matter what you put in it, it's still coffee," he smiled.

He is a really handsome man. His eyes were deep and dark. A perfect nose. The lips were full... his eyes, on me.

I said, "No, it's roast beef, potatoes, wild rice and yams."

He smiled and said, "That's an interesting combination of food."

"I know, I eat strange combinations of food. But, like you say, doesn't really matter how you mix it, it's still food."

He let out a laugh and I found myself laughing with him then I heard myself say, "Would you like to stay for supper? I always make more than I can eat."

He looked at me and smiled, "Yes, I would really enjoy having a sit-down meal with you."

I noticed his hands, they were so delicate looking. "What do you do for a living?" I asked.

He said, "Oh, bit of this and that."

He began talking as I dished out the food. He was telling me some of the funniest things that went on in the community.

After another bite, he said, "One hot day last summer, I came upon Old Fred by the lake. He was lying on his back under his old overturned canvas canoe. One end was propped up on top a saw-horse and that's where he was. He was reaching up trying to glue the frayed end of the canvas. I smelled the strong glue before I noticed a stream of it running from his temple into his hair like some bird crap. Then, when he turned his head to get up I saw that a wad of it has already collected on the back side of his head. I didn't say anything about it. When I saw him again the next day, he looked like a big old grizzly had swiped the scalp down the side of his head. He had running bald spots and a big bald spot at the back where his wife had cut out the glue!"

I just managed to swallow before I laughed out loud.

He continued, "There was another time when Henry's wife was by the shore beside Joe's old canvas canoe. She looked like she was trying to fish something out of the water. She had a long pole with a string and a hook at the end of it. Her long pole began to bend and then I saw a long blade with a short broken wooden handle come up out of the water. She had managed to snag a broken ice chisel. Probably broke and got lost in the snow by the water hole. Anyway, she had this big grin on her face as she grabbed it to examine the long blade. She stood back and her foot turned on the rocky shore and she staggered backward over the canoe. Her hands came down to brace herself and the chisel in her hand—well, she stabbed a hole right through the old canvas canoe. Then, she quickly looked around and pulled an old rag hanging on a branch and slowly put it over the hole and then she turned and ran up the path."

Between the laughter, I managed to ask, "Where were you? Why didn't she see you?"

He answered, "Well, I was sitting up on the rock ledge by the rock cliff to her right. She never thought to look up, I guess."

After a sip of coffee he said, "I think the funniest thing I ever saw though, was that old couple that live by the little creek. You wouldn't believe it but that old man likes to kiss his wife."

I started giggling. I couldn't imagine the old lady kissing the bewhiskered old man. He looked like a very porky walrus.

He continued, "Well, you know he has the big belly and always wears those suspenders to keep his baggy pants up? And, his wife too has a big belly. So, here they are at their wood-pile. He stops in front of her and puts his hands on her arms. Each lean forward after their bellies touch. His lips touch hers, then suddenly, his suspenders snapped at the back and his pants plopped straight down around his ankles."

I was laughing so hard I started coughing.

"Wait, that's not all. He had no shorts on! He was standing there in his hairy bare butt and the old lady was laughing fit to burst and then he leaned over and slowly pulled up his pants. Oh, now that was a most horrible sight to see!"

I was wiping tears from my eyes by this time. I asked, "Did they see you? Where were you?"

He glanced up from his cup of coffee, "Oh, I was coming along on the path when I saw them through the bushes. Well, after that sight, I turned around and went back up the path."

I never knew the people back home were that funny. I guess it takes an outsider to see the inside scoops of humourous situations.

We had just finished the last cup of coffee when he glanced out the window and said, "Oh, there's the tow-truck."

Grabbing his coat, he said, "You will never know how much I enjoyed this. I hope we get the chance to talk again soon. I haven't had so much fun in ages!"

I too, rather enjoyed his company. I walked him to the door. Another wave and then he was running down the street to where I could see the flashing lights of a tow-truck. I came in and closed the door. Then the phone rang.

CHAPTER 8

He had been so careful! He had done all he could to prevent anything from going on with him and Karen. He was really going to make an effort to be clean in heart and body for Janine. He had called and called her number but could not get through. After another week, he had finally got his pelts sold off and he waited for his calls to go through. Finally, in exasperation, he had found himself in Thunder Bay. He had managed to get Janine's mother to give him the address. He smiled now at her reluctance and she had only glanced at the letter lying on the table as an indication to his answer while she was off to get him a cup of tea.

He got to Thunder Bay on a Thursday night and waited around the corner of the old church until he saw her come out of the office building. He had supper at the restaurant on Cumberland Street first and an hour later, he had caught the bus up to Hill Street where he got off and walked down the hill to her apartment corner. He waited around the corner store for a moment until he was sure that she was home. Just then, as he approached, a truck pulled up and a man got out and began to jog down the street, looking at the numbers on the houses. He waited and then he watched him run up the stairs to Charlie's apartment. He memorized the make of the truck and the license plate. He saw the young man go into the porch area and through to the main door. A blind rage seized him as he walked back to the corner store to the telephone booth. He tried to rationalize what the man was doing visiting Janine at her apartment! He waited for a good time that he considered timely for a social visit and then went to the telephone booth on the other side of the store building. Just as he was about to dial the number, he put the phone down. What was he supposed to say? Better calm down first. He went back to the corner store.

Three times, he went to the phone booth without making the call. He was not calming down. If anything, he was getting more and more angry as time went on. Then a tow-truck arrived and parked in front of the man's truck. He walked back out of sight to the telephone again. Finally, he dialed her number. One way or another, he was going to protect her! No man must touch her! Least of all whoever that man was!

He took a deep breath as it rang the third time. He was quite surprised to hear her answer quite calmly and his heart bounced off his chest when he heard her voice.

He managed to say, "Charlie, I miss you terribly and I'm coming to get you. Get your bags packed. You're coming home with me. I need you with me. Please, Charlie. You can't leave me now."

Her voice came again, "Where are you calling me from?"

"Charlie, please don't be angry with me. Can I come to see you?"

"Are you calling from home?"

"I'm in Thunder Bay. I have your address. Got it from your mother's place. It was on the table with your return address on it. I think maybe she left it there on purpose. I went to see her when I came back from the trap-line. I couldn't stay there by myself. I really want you there with me. Please, can I come? I need to talk to you."

* * * *

His voice was shaking; from the cold? He didn't sound drunk. I took a deep breath and leaned against the wall. It was the note I sent mother before Christmas to let her know that I was alright.

Then I heard him say, "Just for a little while."

I asked, "Where are you?"

I felt a jolt of shock run through me when he said, "I'm at the corner store down the street. I'll be there in two minutes. Thanks, Charlie."

In two minutes! He must have ran because I had no sooner sat down at the table to catch my breath when the knock came at the door. My eyes went to the two cups on the table and the two dishes still piled in the sink. He'll see them! I grabbed the cups and threw a cloth over the dirty dishes as another knock came at the door. I opened the door and Freddy entered.

He seemed to fill the whole kitchen as he came in and sat down at the table. I could see his gaze sweeping the counter and the sink and I instantly felt guilty.

"You just finished your supper?"

I stammered a bit as I said, "Yeah, but there's lots left if you'd like to have some."

I quickly did the dishes as he ate what was left of the meal. What would have happened if he had seen Nisha leave? Oh, I felt so scared, like I had almost got caught doing something wrong! I was putting the pan away when I felt his arms come around me. I just stood there as he slowly turned me around, gently kissing my forehead, and he just held me in his arms for the longest time. I could hear his heart beating against my chest. So, now what do I do?

He did all the talking and I went about in a daze as I began packing my things. I had just paid my rent for January. That should be enough notice for the landlord. The more Freddy's voice went on, the more I looked forward to his safe haven; the log cabin along the shoreline of the lake at his trap-line. The cabin was apparently all ready for my arrival. He had gone to the trap-line after I left he says, and prepared the cabin for my return. How did he know I'd come back with him? I had taken all the decorations off the walls when he came and stood in front of me.

He stood smiling down at me for a minute before he said, "I love you, Charlie. I have always loved you."

I looked into the deep brown eyes as his arms came around me. I heard myself say, "I love you too, Freddy."

* * * *

She had come back to him with no more than that. In no more time than that, she was in his arms. He relished his victory and claimed his virgin bride the second time. He reminded himself that he was the only one who had ever touched her. He would keep it that way for as long as he lived! No other man would ever lay a hand on her!

When he had entered her apartment, he saw immediately that the pip-squeak had supper with Janine. The dishes were still at the sink, but as he later checked out the place, he saw that the bed was still neatly made and that satisfied him. He slept on the couch that night at her apartment. He vowed he would not touch her again until she was at his cabin at the trap-line.

They managed to get a ride to Armstrong and then caught the train to the community where Janine barely had time to run to see her mother for a few minutes before he swung by there with the snow machine all loaded up for the trip to the trap-line. He promised himself that he would take it easy with his drinking until she got used to him. Well, the way things were, it was pretty hard for him to face the community. Him, being the rogue claiming the princess of the community. He saw her as someone so... well, just so good, so beautiful, so... sinless, like an angel seemingly untouched by all the ugliness of life, poverty, and lawlessness.

He had watched her closely since she was a child. As soon as he was told that she would be his wife, he had watched her. He saw her hauling water for the old man who was so sick with a hangover. He had watched her and Al fish the little animals in the sack out of the water at the edge of the dock. He had watched her shoot slingshots with Tom and Dave. Oh, she was a good shot with the thing. Then, he had watched her cry by the stream when she had found so many too-small suckers that the boys had left to rot on the shoreline.

She was a strange girl indeed, and he loved her all the more for it. Only once had he had the nerve to approach her when she was crying and in answer to his question she had yelled, "I hit him! Many times! I hit him because he said bad things about his mother!" He had laughed because she was feeling sad for beating up Al because he tried to hit her as his father always hit his mother. Suddenly, he was the bad guy because he had laughed! Oh, girls were hard to understand! Now, she was a woman and a beautiful one at that.

How was he to keep her from getting mad at him? To love her. That was the answer. When she understood how much he loved her and what pains he had gone through to make her comfortable, what more could she ask? He loved her and he would make her his princess. He was going to make sure that she would be a perfectly contented wife and live like a queen in the cabin in the woods. He would make her become a part of the land; his life. He would provide everything she had grown accustomed to and she would not go without. That was all that she would need for him to show her how much he loved her.

CHAPTER 9

It was with such immense love that I watched Fred from the window, throwing the logs off the sleigh behind the snow machine. He suddenly turned and waved. I waved back. How did he know I was watching him? The cabin was very warm and cozy. I had just finished frying some fish. The rice and the bannock were already on the table. He'd be in soon. I stood by the table and smoothed down my apron. Then I heard his footsteps coming down the path to the doorstep and then he was in the room. The small cabin felt so empty when he was out. As always, he immediately hung his coat and turned to the sink behind the door to wash up. Then he came and gave me a big hug and a kiss. I loved the smell of him, the taste of him, and he was all mine.

I found it hard to believe that we had been here for almost three months. It felt like such a very short time. We had not returned to the village yet and I had no wish to. I'd like it if we stayed here forever, all by ourselves. But I know he wanted to go to town soon. If we were to stay here over spring break-up, we'd have to stock up on food supplies. I didn't want to stay in the village while we waited for the ice to go. I'd rather stay here in our little cabin. But I'd have to go with him to get the groceries because I didn't want to stay here by myself.

"Now what's put that expression on your face, luv?"

He brushed my forehead with a kiss as he sat down beside me on the bench. I kept my eyes on the beautiful view of the lake as he talked about the trip to the community the day after tomorrow. It would be a weekend trip. I hated the thought of a weekend trip. What would happen while we were there? I wished I had my notepad.

"What are you doing this afternoon?"

He smiled as he slowly chewed on his food. I knew I was a good cook and he loved what I cooked. I had learned quick to memorize recipes at the apartment after I got so sick of bologna and macaroni in tomato sauce.

"Check my rabbit snares." I smiled back at him.

After all this time, I still felt shy at times. I just couldn't believe that this big hunk of a man was mine. My husband... strange word.

He'd be at the wood-pile all day. After he finished hauling the wood here, he'd get the power-saw going and saw the logs to short pieces to fit the stove and then he'd split all the wood and stack them beside the cabin wall and bring some inside as well. I learned to just stay out of the way when he worked with the wood. He made me feel so inadequate, like a bumbling idiot when I was with him out there. I felt so embarrassed and my knees shook when I felt him looking at me. The first week we were out here, I was trying to figure out what he wanted me to do or what I was supposed to do. I soon found out that every time I tried to do something that he did not want me to do anyway, I always goofed up! Like the time I tripped on a branch and nearly fell on the power-saw, the first time I accompanied him to cut down the trees. Another time, the axe head fell off the handle and just missed my head. And then there was the time I slipped on a piece of wood and landed close to the chopping block just as his axe came down. That was it, he declared the wood site out of bounds for me.

He made me feel like I was invading his territory if I was with him while he worked. But, I accompanied him to check the nearby traps and whatever else needed to be done, when he'd let me. Otherwise, he'd tell me what needed to be done at the cabin, or suggested what I should be doing instead. I never objected or took offense to anything. I smiled and agreed. In that way, we had a lot of fun. I loved to hear him laugh. I didn't mind being left at the cabin at times. How else was I going to get any work done? I got the bed made and tidied up as he came and went around the cabin. At those times when he checked his trap-lines further out, I did the laundry or scrubbed the floor. I always rushed to get all my work done before he came home. He'd come home to see clothes and sheets hanging on the line. The next time, he'd come home to find them gone. Always, the cabin was neat and tidy and there was always the smell of something delicious cooking. I made a point of never having him catch me doing anything. For some reason, I got very embarrassed if he saw me working. So, I made sure that I got all my work done before he came home.

There was one day when there was such a bad storm outside that he stayed inside the whole time. I felt so uncomfortable and embarrassed as he watched my every move as I washed the dishes and prepared the meals. It was all I could do that day. I even hated to go the outhouse because I knew he'd know where I'd been.

When we first arrived, I was so embarrassed when I first went into the outhouse and realized that he had nailed on a brand new toilet seat just for me! A pink toilet seat! I felt ready to crawl into the hole myself! I smiled at the cabin when I first saw it. Everything was all mis-matched but my heart melted at his attempt to make it nice and homey for me, as he said. I really didn't know how long I could do this... this playhouse game he was playing. He insisted on this in the way he talked and did things, that this was how he wanted things to be. This was how and what he wanted me to be. The problem was that the role I was playing was not really me!

"I guess this is one of your quiet days, eh? What are you thinking about?" He nudged me as he sipped the hot tea.

"I was just thinking about town. I hate to go but I don't want to stay here by myself either."

"Now, you don't want to go because you don't know where we will stay. Is that it? Well, we're not going to your mother's so don't worry about that. I paid Sheila and Bob to fix up my family's old shack the last time I was down there, so we can stay there if you'd like."

His family's old shack was the last one to the west shore. That might be nice. Suddenly, I felt a lot better as I picked up the dishes and began clearing the table. Fred was back outside again. Soon, the power-saw would start. Compared to the normal peaceful silence, it was so noisy, you couldn't hear yourself think! I grabbed my coat, dressed up warm and left the cabin.

I took my time checking the rabbit snares that I had set along the shore. Every once in a while, I smelled the wood smoke from the cabin. I watched a woodpecker on an old poplar tree. He seemed so intent banging his head against the tree that he didn't even pause as I walked by. The chickadees and jays were quite indignant at my having disturbed their business as I quietly walked by along the shore. I walked in the shade of the trees. That was when I first saw it. A lone black wolf. He seemed to just materialize at the point in front of me and then, he was gone. I turned around. The sun was now about to go down over the horizon. I couldn't wait to see what this place looked like in the summer. He said there was a beach where he had his canoe hung up on the racks.

After a while, I began to notice that there was no sound of the power-saw within hearing distance as I ran along the snare trail in my moccasins. I should be able to hear it. I did the last time I came this way while he was cutting the wood. Maybe, he got hurt! I ran as fast as I could back to the cabin.

I came running around the corner only to see Fred sitting on the wood-pile. The power-saw had broken down and I knew he did not have enough money to buy another one until the next batch of furs were sold. He had not intended to do that until spring. I remembered the five hundred dollars I still had in the bank in Sioux Lookout. I watched the back of his head when I mentioned the money I had in the bank. He would have none of it and seemed offended that I would suggest such a thing. He threw the axe on the wood-pile and stomped into the cabin.

We arrived at the community late at night and drove the snow machine right up to the door of the old shack. When the match was lit, I was surprised to see curtains at the windows and blankets on the bed. It was rather quite nice! There was even a table cloth on the square rough wooden table.

We had just got the fire going when we heard a snow machine coming and a woman's voice laughing with a man's voice yelling over the noise of the machine. The machine stopped outside and the door opened. Bob and Sheila walked in. She had a pot of stew and Bob had some pop and a whiskey bottle.

I glanced apprehensively at the bottle, thinking, well, here we go. A cup was shoved into my hand. It had the pop and some of the stuff from the bottle in it. It didn't taste quite so bad. We laughed and talked into the night. Fred had us all laughing, telling them about my escapades in the trap-line. When the sun was tinting the horizon, the couple left and we crawled into bed. I fell asleep thinking this was really nice.

The next morning, we got on the morning train to Savant Lake after a quick breakfast of scrambled eggs and bannock at Bob and Sheila's place next door. I never knew Bob that well and Sheila was his new second wife. She had just moved in with him last year. It was with great relief that they turned out to be a very nice couple.

Fred stayed beside me on the train and throughout the day in Savant Lake as we packed boxes of food and supplies. I couldn't resist buying the newspapers and a few magazines. Just before the train came in, Fred ducked into the liquor store. I watched him disappear inside with dismay. Maybe, he wasn't buying it for himself. I had noticed that he had a habit of buying liquor for others in the community. I've known him to go and give a bottle to the old man at the end of the road from his cabin. He came out with a bag under his arm and with that, we got on the train back to the village.

This time, right after we gave our tickets to the conductor, he kissed my forehead as he got up and said, "I won't be long."

He went to the Club Car and I sat by myself all the way back home. I got a newspaper from a passenger several seats from me and I read every single article before we got to the village.

Fred came along just as the train was slowing to a stop and we got off. Bob was there already with the sleigh and snow machine. They loaded the sleigh and Fred and I drove off to the cabin with Bob yelling that they'd be right over. We had just finished bringing in all the boxes when the people began arriving. One after the other, people from the community came and went, with each getting a swig from the bottle that Fred had bought. I had noticed that he gave two of the bottles to Bob. He had three in the box, now there was only one left. Soon, the crowd began thinning out and then Mother and O arrived. Fred had been drinking with the people and now he was beginning to show some effects. I had also taken the cup from him several times and noticed that I was feeling rather... well, just like the night before. After some rough moments, O began to be a bit more civil when another cup was pressed into his hand. Then Bob and Sheila arrived with the other bottles.

It was getting dark and I lit the lamp. After awhile the traffic thinned out and I went out to the outhouse with Sheila. We laughed out loud and howled as she joked about a neighbour of theirs. I laughed out loud again as I watched Sheila dancing, waiting for her turn at the toilet. She was such a good friend. I laughed as she told me things about Bob and the others in the community. It had taken me awhile to realize that this was like a wedding celebration. That's why the people were coming in like that, to greet us and wishing us well. My wedding... Hmmph!

Out of the shivering cold, Sheila and I came into the cabin in a cloud of mist. It was around eleven o'clock when I was right in the middle of laughing that I felt Bob's hand slide down my back. I caught Fred's eye and I went to brush past Bob to get to the other side of the room when he pulled me and I slid on to his lap. With both Bob's arms around me now, I saw the murderous gaze from Fred across the room by the table. Sheila was babbling on about something to Fred and Mother was busy arguing with my step-father. In all the chaos, I was struggling to get up and away from Bob's hands when Freddy's chair crashed to the floor. Fred was standing in the middle of the floor and yelling for everyone to get out! I watched Mother and O stagger out the door as I came and stood beside Fred.

I kept muttering, "Why? What are you doing?"

He yelled, "Get out! Get out!" as Bob and Sheila hurried out.

Then silence filled the room. I had never seen Freddy so angry! I didn't know what to do or what to say.

I asked, "What's the matter Fred?"

Suddenly, I went flying across the room and fell with a crash across the bed. Then, I heard the door slam shut. A deep burning sting was starting across my face. He had hit me! Freddy slapped me! In the silence of the cabin, I started to sob uncontrollably. I couldn't believe what had happened, and how quickly!

I woke up freezing cold. It was morning and the fire had gone out. He never came home. Where had he gone? I remembered he had just turned and ran out the door in his rage. Where could he have gone? Maybe to that woman with the two kids.

Fuelled by my own anger I got the fire going and made myself a strong cup of coffee. After my second cup and still pacing the floor, I decided to go and look for him. I dressed warm and washed by face in the porcelain sink behind the door. My hands froze as I gazed into the little four-by-four inch square mirror hanging above the sink. Oh, my gosh! I still had a red mark that went across my cheek. I slowly sank to the floor thinking that this was going to stop right now! I had to leave right now! If I stayed, it would never end. But, where would I go? I don't have an apartment in the city anymore. Oh, my darling Fred! Why have you done this! Oh, Fred, where are you? Where was he?

Suddenly I got up and rummaged through my cosmetics bag. I put on some make-up but there wasn't much I could do with my puffy eyes from all my crying last night, so I grabbed the dark sun-glasses I wore when we went checking traps in the bright sunshine against the snow. I slammed the door and started down the path. Where should I go? I got as far as Bob and Sheila's place when I heard a yell.

CHAPTER 10

Oh, it had been a pretty rough couple of months! He had done his very best but it wasn't enough. He soon found that she was absolutely clumsy and unfit for bush life! He had to keep the fire going day and night for her. All she was willing to do was to keep the cabin nice and tidy and smelling of home-cooked food. No, the problem wasn't that! Heaven knows how appreciative he was of her cooking. Now, here he had to give her credit. She could turn the most basic of ingredients into great gourmet dishes. That was part of the problem that was bothering him though. It was like he was sitting down to a gourmet meal every evening! He wished for a more relaxed meal without steak knives, butter knives, forks and spoons. Why did he have to buy the darned things for in the first place! Just once, he yearned for a big pot of rabbit stew where he could chomp through all the parts of the animal and damn the frozen veggies!

He was beginning to tire of the playhouse game they were into. Who did she think she was anyway? All he wanted was food to eat! He only used to light the stove when he was hungry or had anything to cook, now it was on full speed, day and night! It kept him at it full time now, day and night, just getting the wood ready everyday for the next day!

Then there was her English. She spoke perfect English; the proper school marm English! He often wondered if he'd ever get used to speaking English all the time! He had tried many times to speak to her in Ojibway only to have her answer in her no-accent proper English.

Then there was that one evening in particular that he remembered when she had grabbed a roll of toilet paper from the table and blew her nose hard then she suddenly leaned over going, "Oh, yuk!" and spitting into the slop pail.

"What? Bleeding nose?" he had asked.

"No," she had exclaimed, "I blew too hard and it bounced off the paper and went into my mouth!"

Why didn't she just say "snot" he had wondered.

He had turned to the wall saying, "Sorry that we ran out of Kleenex."

She had said nothing more and began tidying up.

Toilet paper and tissues were the other things that he had never had to stock up on before. This was harder than he had thought. He just wanted to relax and be himself but he was stuck with this monster he had created. He wondered if she was like that all the time or how long she would stay like this? Never once did she let her guard down. It was like he was watching her performing. She was so out of place! It was like he had plucked her out of her city apartment and plunked her into the trapper's shack and she went about her daily business as if nothing had changed! Wait, now. Wasn't that what he wanted her to be? Yes, but not like this! It was like her spirit wasn't in it. She never let on what she was feeling. She never said anything about anything! The aprons looked good on her though. He had thought to throw them into his shopping pile at the last minute. She always had one on when she was cooking. She was so beautiful. What had he done?

When they went into town, he swore he would make a great effort to stay civilized. He vowed he'd try his best to please her. But, when they got to Savant Lake, she made a bee-line for a newspaper and he watched her buying food and supplies that he never used to eat or use. It was as if she had no thought for him. She never even made a comment about the nice cabin. She was taking over his life and he was getting nothing back! So, on the spur of the moment, he bought the liquor. He felt he was entitled to a bit of fun and some of his own life back. And so, the drinking had started. He had seen that Bob was getting too friendly and Janine had only laughed. She had laughed! She had tormented him! He loved her but there was evidently no love for him. He drank and drank and he did not remember the blind rage... and then, he was in Karen's warm embrace on her kitchen floor. As always though, when he drank, he immediately fell asleep. Karen always said that she would always make sure he fell asleep in her loving arms and not in the snow to freeze to death whenever he was in town.

It was early morning when he awoke and decided to go and talk to the Priest. He had to find a way to keep Janine beside him. He had walked across the tracks and down to the Priest's cabin before he realized that he left his coat at Karen's place. After a conversation with the Priest of which he wasn't quite sure what they spoke about, he later awoke with his head on the Priest's table and then hurried back to Karen's to retrieve his jacket from the back of the kitchen chair. Karen was still fast asleep between her little children on the double bed. He had decided not to awaken her to thank her for letting him sleep on her kitchen floor.

It was as he had crossed the railroad tracks and was coming over the hill when he saw Janine. Again, instant rage had filled him as he thought, "What was she doing by Bob's place so early in the morning? Was she coming from there?"

* * * *

I glanced to the sound of his voice and felt an excruciating emotional pain well up to choke me. I watched Fred coming over the hill from that woman's place! He was coming from Karen's place! I turned and started running towards him. How dare he! He still looked very angry as I approached him.

He stopped and said, "So, you're on your way to Bob's for more?"

How dare he! Suddenly, my arm shot out, grabbed the glasses off my face and with my other hand, I punched him as hard as I could in the belly. He staggered back and then grabbing his middle, he bent over and promptly threw up all over his boots. I stood perfectly still as he stood retching and I watched the vomit slide over his boots and into the snow.

He gasped, "Why'd you do that for?"

Then, still angry, I said, "That was for thinking such an awful thing of me and that was for knowing where you are just coming from, and that was for... no I should hit you as hard as I can a couple more times for hitting me last night. Look at me! Don't you ever, ever hit me again! Do you hear me? Look what you did to me!"

He stood blinking at me for several seconds before he whispered, as if he was coming out from a deep shock, "I hit you? I hit you? Oh, my gosh, I really did hit you didn't I? Oh, luv I'm so sorry. I'm sorry, Charlie. I never meant to hurt you. I must never hurt you. Oh, God! I have never hit a woman in my whole life! I'll never, never, touch you in anger again, luv. I'm so sorry! Please forgive me. Oh god, Janine, I'm so sorry."

He looked like a walking zombie with his arms outstretched beseechingly, as he lunged toward me, "I'm sorry luv, I'm so sorry luv."

I felt his arms close around me. We stood there rocking side to side as tears rained over my face, before I turned and we walked back to the cabin with our arms around each other. The hopelessness of it all just totally overwhelmed me. I could not see any way out of this situation. I loved him dearly but I was choking to death in its suffocating depth!

We had just sat down at the table when I said, "You must tell me where you were last night or I'll keep wondering if..."

His hand stopped as his coffee cup was on its way to his mouth. After a few seconds, he smiled and took a sip of coffee and said, "I went to see the Priest. I woke up there this morning and came along the railroad tracks and across the hill. I guess I didn't want to walk by Bob's place."

I looked at him trying to gauge if he was serious.

"Why would you want to see the Priest?"

"I guess I figured that you may not be so free to leave me if I married you, in the church, I mean," he said with a smile.

I said nothing as the information registered in my brain. He was afraid of me leaving? He was willing to marry me just so I wouldn't leave him? I had always thought that a man proposed to the woman if he loved her enough to marry her!

Nothing more was said as we began to re-pack the things we had bought. When I thought we were about ready, I decided to go and visit my mother before we left. I was about half way there when the twins, Lenny and Benny, came running behind me. One was jabbering about last night saying that they couldn't even get in the door to see me. And, had I been drinking? They had heard me laughing.

Then one of them said, "Then later on we came back when we saw Fred at Karen's place but there was no light at your place."

I stopped still and turned around.

"What did you say? When was Fred at Karen's place? What time was it?"

The taller one, Benny, said, "Oh, I don't know. We were looking for mom and dad and we heard noise at Karen's so we went there. But they weren't there, just Fred and some other people."

I turned right around and headed back down the path to the Priest's house. I knocked on the door. It was afternoon now and the door opened before I could knock again. The Priest smiled as he bid me to enter.

I stopped just inside the door and asked, "Would you tell me please, about what time did Freddy leave this morning?"

"Oh," the Priest stopped to think, "He came in around five o'clock, such an early hour, and then he dozed off and then he left when he woke around eight o'clock, I think."

Then where was he the rest of the night?

"Thank you."

I turned to go when he said, "Wait now, you did not ask what he came to see me about."

I smiled, "If you'll remember Father, I am Anglican. Goodbye, Father and thank-you."

I turned and closed the door behind me. The Groundhogs were still standing there by the door, waiting for me. I had no idea what time it was when Fred came over the hill. I never thought to look at my watch when I decided to go and look for him. I could ask around and sound ridiculously like a jealous wife. I just have to forget it and think that they weren't left alone during the night. I kicked at the snow as I walked to my mother's cabin thinking how I hated this place and all the people in it!

When I got back to Fred's cabin again, it was to find him in his best clothes all ready to go to town, never mind his snowsuit for the trap-line, he had on his town coat.

"Where are you going all dressed like that?" I asked.

He smiled and he said, "We, not I. We are going to Sioux Lookout. I decided we could use your money and buy that power-saw after all. I can't see us spending the next three months with just the axe and hand-saw. I'll be at the wood-pile all day long, every single day just to keep you warm, if that's the case."

Although he said it with a smile, I did not like the sound of it. I was the cause of keeping the fire going? I was the cause of all his hard work? I thought that was what he normally did. Why was it my fault that he had to cut wood? Did he not keep the fire going when he was home? Well, if it was my fault, then I would pay for the damn power-saw! But then there goes my ticket out money.

The east-bound train would be arriving soon and all I had time for was to grab my winter coat and change my boots. We ran to the station just as the train was coming to a stop. After we paid for the tickets, Fred got up and left me. I never saw him again, until he came and pushed me across to the window seat hours later when the train stopped in Sioux Lookout. I didn't like this.

We had no sooner checked into the room when he turned and went downstairs. I figured he'd be in the bar until closing time around one o'clock in the morning. I went out and had supper at the same restaurant and at the same table where I was when he first came and sat down across from me last fall. Now, where was he? He was in the bar probably with the same woman!

I finished my meal and went back into the hotel. I slowed down as I made my way up the stairs. I was sure someone was in our room. As I approached the door, it was suddenly flung open and there was Fred, very drunk and very angry about something. I never even had time to say anything before he grabbed me by the coat and flung me on the bed. I curled up wondering what he was going to do. He kept pacing back and forth across the floor yelling.

"Where the heck have you been? Eh? Where did you disappear to the minute I turned my back? Eh?"

He kept yelling the same question over and over again, getting more and more angry.

I finally yelled back, "I went to the restaurant for supper!"

Now he was standing over me, his face about a foot away from mine. "Then why didn't you let me know, eh? Why didn't you invite me out to supper, eh? You always act like you are better than me, you know that?"

I yanked off my coat and pulled the blanket over me saying, "Stop yelling at me and stop spitting into my face when you talk!"

He took one long hard look at me, took a deep breath and suddenly he whirled around and stomped into the bathroom, slamming the door behind him.

I lay perfectly still, wondering what he was doing in there. After about half an hour, he came out of the bathroom and sank down on the bed beside me. He lay his head on my shoulder and I listened to his anguished sobs until he was able to speak. My brain numbly registered what he was saying. I was in totally unknown territory. I had absolutely no idea what to do or say. I lay motionless, silently listening. He begged for forgiveness and tried to explain what was happening to him. What he was feeling. What he had been feeling. That he loved me now more than anything or anyone else in the whole world. If only I would care. If only I could love him as much.

He had his arm around me and begged that I should let him know that I loved him as much as he loved me. Yes, he could be right. I may not have shown him how much I too loved him. I don't remember being able to hug him out of the blue like he always did with me. I never knew how to. I remembered Linda. She would understand. She would straighten out all this mess and tell me exactly what I needed to do without actually telling me. No, I had never actually shown him how much I loved him. I had only actually told him just that once at the apartment that time when he came and got me. I knew I wasn't much good at such things. Yes, perhaps I did or said things that I would normally do or say in the city that would make him think that perhaps I thought I was better than he was. But, I was only trying to be the person he thought I was or wanted me to be. Yes, I perhaps didn't change as much as he had tried to change since we had been together. Yes, I should work harder. I'll try harder.

I began to stroke his head. I bent and kissed the top of his head. I told him that I loved him very much. That I would tell him how much I loved him, every day. Yes, I would try to be a better wife to him. I assured him that I was only doing my best to be what he thought I was. Suddenly, I felt very nauseous. I hated this.

*   *   *   *

Begging for forgiveness was the best thing to do. He didn't want to give her another excuse that would cause her to pack her things and walk out on him again. He was always in dread that she would just walk out. She had money stashed at the bank. But, at how many banks?

It was just getting daylight when he awoke with a splitting headache. He looked at her shadowed face and heard her breathing softly. He slowly made his way to the bathroom and closed it quietly behind him. He was feeling utterly sick as he splashed water on his face. Oh, he looked terrible! Yesterday, when he realized he had slapped her, he in his own way, had asked her to marry him and she had just looked at him as if wondering why he would say such a thing! Then she had just left the cabin without a word to see her mother. She had been gone an awful long time at which time he had decided that if she spent some of her own money on the trap-line things, then maybe she'd have a bit more respect with the supplies. He would use her money to get the power-saw.

She took the news without comment as if nothing he did ever made any difference to her! He spent the trip to Sioux Lookout in the Club Car to avoid any bad words with her. He felt it was better to stay away from her than risk saying something that would hurt her still further.

It was when he was coming back to his seat just before the train reached Sioux Lookout that he saw her head leaning over to talk to the red-haired man beside her on the opposite seat across the aisle. He too had his head out toward her, waving his arms around to the conversation. He had stopped several seats back and caught bits and pieces of the conversation through the clickity-clack of the train. They were in some discussion about world trade or some such thing. He had been swept with such rage that she would talk like that and not mind her place! He was feeling such a wave of betrayal, embarrassment, and then finally, the fury that he hadn't a clue what they had been talking about! She was like them and he was excluded! She would never be like him!

When they got to the hotel, he had gone downstairs for a drink when he ran into Gladys. He was in the process of telling her not to come knocking on his door when she began laughing and said that she had just seen his lady friend slipping out with a man she was seen with her several times before when she had been in town. He had rushed upstairs only to find Janine gone. He began to get absolutely furious as the minutes ticked by. By the time he heard her approaching the door, he was in a blind rage. Had he not been drinking, he would have known that Janine would never do such a thing! Only women like Gladys did such things! Gladys that bitch! She did it on purpose. It was her payback and he fell for it. How she must have laughed!

CHAPTER 11

I was at the bank the next day. He stood behind me as I filled out the withdrawal form. Quite instinctively, I left one hundred dollars in the account. I never told him exactly how much I had in there. I never told him that I also had money in the bank in Thunder Bay. It was my out money and it would stay there no matter what. I handed him the four hundred dollars. I hadn't said much since I disentangled myself from his arms and legs earlier that morning. The train would be here soon.

I watched him buy the power-saw at the store and we boarded the train for home within the hour. This time, he stayed beside me all the way to the village and I sat looking out the window, wondering how long I was going to last in this situation. My only hope was that we would get to the trap-line before something else happened. I didn't even want to see my mother. I could just imagine what she would say. Maybe I could think of an excuse or something. Once out in the trap-line, I'll have to decide how I am going to handle the next stage. I did not want a baby, but I did not have time to find a doctor for birth control pills. I wish I could get him to talk. But, he just looks at me with that closed face of his and that's when my mouth clamps shut and my tongue lies still. Only my brain reacts with silent comments, screams, questions, and perhaps some hopeless suggestions as to what to do next. I glanced at him and a shock went though me as I watched a tear slowly making its way down his cheek as he looked out the window. I looked away. My heart continued to beat very hard for the next while. I hadn't a clue what to do.

We returned to the cabin by the lake at the trap-line. The emotional pain remained deep inside my chest for a good month before I began to respond to Fred's loving attention. We watched the ice recede and we went hunting when the ducks arrived. We tied the canoe on top the sleigh behind the snow machine and loaded the canoe up with all our camping supplies. We managed to take the snow machine as far as we could to the mouth of the river where we decided to set up camp at a point. We shovelled the snow off an area for the tent and the snow piled beside the entrance became my freezer. Every time he killed a duck, I cleaned and prepared it, I dug out a little snowy compartment in the snowbank and shoved the duck into it and packed it up closed with snow. It was here that one morning as I shoved another duck into the snow pile when I heard him laughing softly behind me.

I whirled around laughing and demanding, "What are you laughing at?"

He had just returned from a firewood trip and he stood there, swinging the axe back and forth in his hand before he said, "You forgot something. You're supposed to leave a stick sticking out of each spot so you don't loose the spot where you buried one!"

I looked apprehensively at the bank thinking, oh, now wait a minute, it's not like I had buried them all over the camp-site, I have them all between the end of the tent wall and the poplar tree. Now, how could I possibly lose any? But, about a few weeks later when we moved to another site, he sat by the fire laughing at me when I could only find twelve of the fourteen ducks that I had buried! I was still moving the snow all around the camp-site trying to find the two ducks before he finally persuaded me that perhaps I had miscounted. I thought myself a failure! It was at this time that I began to get very nauseous in the mornings.

My love for Fred deepened as he pampered me in the coming days and weeks. We knew I was pregnant. I was determined to forget the ugliness that had happened when we went into town. I treasured the days and weeks we spent together in peace and gentle loving kindness.

I got up very early one morning when we were no more than one hour's paddle away from the cabin down river from the spring hunting site. I had been so violently awaken with nausea that I had barely made it over to the wood-pile where I wretched as quietly as I could. I thought he was still asleep inside the tent and I was quite startled upon coming back, when I saw him by the water. I felt a shiver run clear down my back to my toes when I realized he was deliberately waving his arms to the left and right, in front of him and behind him. In his hand he held a pipe. I never even knew he had a pipe! I could hear his voice, an intonation. I could not hear any words. For some reason, fear and embarrassment came over me. I did not know anything like this about him. I wasn't aware people still did things like that. I thought it was only when they were drunk that they would sing their wailing sad songs. He was praying! I thought only the old Indians used to do that. I wasn't aware anyone still did that! How? Why? What else did I not know about this man?

I was back in bed when he returned. He got the tiny wood-stove going full blast and I waited for the tent to heat up while he made some coffee. He never said anything about the song or the pipe and I never asked any questions or made any comment whatsoever. Now, when I knew he was going off alone, I stayed well away from the area and, I got lost once.

I got lost, as lost as any idiot in the bush could be! He had gone down the river in the canoe alone as I didn't relish the idea of barfing over the side of the canoe! Being left alone, I took the old .22 and went in search of a partridge. I had no sooner cleared the wood-pile when I saw one. I had the sight on him when I stopped as a wave of nausea washed over me. The partridge was still there when I lifted my head again and I lined up the sight and pulled the trigger. The partridge went down with a flutter of wings, beating desperately against the mossy ground. It hobbled and flopped its wings into the dense bush. I crept forward but as soon as it became quiet long enough for me to put the sights of the gun on it again, it suddenly flapped its wings and disappeared under another bush. In this way, I chased it quite deep into the swamp where every footprint popped up out of the smooth fluffy absorbent moss that left no tracks behind me!

After another shot, I crawled under an overhanging old tree and saw the partridge beneath a branch. I stopped and fired. This time it wasn't quite quick enough to have lead me further in. Now, I was standing in the middle of the swamp plucking the feathers off the partridge, slowly turning around and around, and finally came to a stop when I realized that I had absolutely no idea which direction I had come from! How many times had Mom told us about the trickster. The partridge who would lead us to get lost in the swamp if we attempted to kill her or her babies. I had fallen for the old trick. After being warned about it over and over again by Mom from the time I could remember, I had gone ahead and done it! I couldn't believe it. I stood there in the middle of the swamp, head hanging in shame when I heard the twelve-gauge shots echoing all around me.

My heart jumped! Fred! I could not tell where the shots came from because the noise echoed all around from the poplar and pine trees standing like sentries. I had no idea whether it came from the left, right, front, or back! Then another shot rang out in the distance, although it soon bounced all around me, I kept in the direction of the trees where I first heard it. I thanked those trees as I rushed forward now, unceremoniously smashing the partridge against logs and moss covered rocks to gain balance as I ran, skipping and hopping full speed through the swamp and bush, over and under fallen logs and tree trunks until I emerged well behind the last wood-pile by the river. I saw no trace of Fred.

I hurried to the campfire and built it up. I threw up behind the wood-pile before putting the tea pot on the fire and another pot for the partridge. I was going to make partridge and dumpling stew tonight. I was laying back against a block of wood beside the campfire in total contentment when I heard the swish, splash of his paddle against the quiet spring evening with the sound of ducks settling down for the night.

My mind kept drifting to that scene of Fred against the early morning light. What was that ceremony of some kind that I had seen him do? There was no such thing that I could remember in our family. These things were done quietly, inconspicuously during the course of the day, according respect to the birds, animals, and plants, at all times without a big fanfare, recognizing their more predominant importance by respecting them without attracting attention to one self. I decided not to say anything about it. Did he think that I did not know? Or, was he hoping that I would chance to see him? Most likely though, was that he did not care if I did or not.

After that spring, we went into summer where I was quite content to float around in luxury in the water by the sand beach around the point from our boat landing. He was still hauling logs for the tourist camp at the other end of the lake where they were going to build an ice house or something. I was basking in love and happiness deciding that no one or anything was going to disrupt my little piece of heaven on earth.

I listened to songs full blast on my small portable record player perched on a rock as I lay spread out with my growing belly floating to the sun. I smiled and closed my eyes. That was the best of my summer months.

It was on a very hot day in August that Fred suddenly decided he was going to take me to visit his favourite aunt at a Reserve up north. I was very excited about visiting. I had not met any of his relatives so far and I wanted to feel like a part of his family too. Fred ordered a plane from the tourist camp and we flew out directly from our cabin. After about an hour, we landed at the Reserve. We walked through two streets before he turned to one of the identically built houses.

"Hey, Gook!" he yelled as we entered.

From around the corner, a woman appeared. She had a long red and blue checkered dress on and a blue sweater buttoned to the neck. Her wrinkled face broke into a big smile as Fred swept her into his arms. Then she turned to me and touched my arm as her face wrinkled into a big smile. Fred took our two boxes to the other bedroom as he was directed. I knew it was going to be a nice visit.

But then, about an hour later, I was quite surprised when Fred suddenly announced that he was flying back to town to get some shopping done and that he'd be back in a week. With no more than just a pat on the arm, he was out the door and down the street! Later, we heard the plane take off again. He was gone. He had left me here all alone! Gull darn it, why does he do that! In one minute, he had undone all that I thought we had built up in the past months!

The days came and went. One week went by and then another. I alternated between anger and worry. What had happened to him? Where was he? How could he just leave me like this! I took to borrowing Gook's canoe when she wasn't up to accompanying me on my endless paddles along the shoreline. I couldn't stand the wait, anxiously looking down the street every time I heard a plane land.

I returned one evening and found a little boy about five years old sitting on Gook's lap. I remembered then that she had been expecting him. Her grandchild had arrived. The mother had dropped him off and left again on the same plane. He was a skinny little boy with deep sparkling eyes and his name was Remy. He apparently came to stay with her every summer. "Gook" I discovered was short for Gookom, my grandma.

Several days later, I listened to her yelling at the boy, "Don't go out the window if you came in through the door. Go out the same way you came in!"

The boy asked, "Why?"

Gook heaved a sigh and said, "Because of the people in the room. You will tie their lives in knots when you do that!"

I remembered my mother saying that many times. As a child, I had thought about that, trying to figure out what it might mean, but the boy just shrugged and he was gone again. I smiled to myself.

One night Remy and his buddy, who looked to be about seven years old, built a tent beside the house where they were going to sleep that night. The little tent was right under Gook's window.

I heard her saying in a hushed voice, "Don't look at the northern lights."

I heard the boy's voice ring out, "Why, Gook?"

Gook stuck her head out the window again and said, "Because they will come down and get you! And don't whistle to them either!"

The boy's voice came again, "Why, Gook?"

Gook heaved a sigh and said, "Those are ghosts dancing up there and they will start to dance faster and faster if you whistle to them, and then suddenly they will swoop down and get you. When they come to get you, you will begin to hear a loud swishing sound and it will get louder and louder and then you won't be able to move, and then they will swoop you up!"

I smiled as I sat at the kitchen table thinking, yes, I had heard all about the northern lights too. Where will I be when I tell my child such things? My heart was so heavy and although my morning sickness was gone, I suffered from heartburn most of the time. What was I going to do? What now? Is this what he will do every time he wanted to go to town and party with the women? Is this what it will be like for the rest of my life? I will have one baby after another while my husband just takes off any time he likes without explanation, and expect to find me exactly where he left me? I felt used. I felt trapped. I felt very angry. Then, I felt helpless and victimized.

One day just as the sun was setting, Remy came running into the kitchen where Gook was preparing fish for supper, yelling in English, "Look, Gook! There's a cloud with a curly golden wig!"

I chuckled about that and glanced at Gook. She was trying so hard to get him to speak in Ojibway.

She looked out the window and said slowly in Ojibway, "Oh, so it is. What once was normal, looks kind of strange now, doesn't it? Just an old cloud dressing up fancy!"

The boy fixed his gaze on her face for a full minute without saying a word before he whirled around and dashed out of the house again.

It was exactly three weeks and two days when I happened to glance out the window and my knees became weak. There was Fred coming down the street. I hadn't even heard the plane land. When he came in, he came toward me and gave me a quick hug. He smelled strange and he looked a lot thinner. There was no explanation other than that it was just the length of time it took him to get done what he needed to do. I didn't ask what that might have been. As far as I knew, we only needed some groceries, canvas, nails and paint for the old canvas canoe that he wanted to re-cover! I deliberately kept my distance. I moved away when he tried to reach for me in the single bed he shared with me that night.

With promises to come and visit us, we said our goodbyes to Gook and Remy the next day, and flew out directly back to our trap-line.

CHAPTER 12

As I approached the cabin, everything seemed as I had left it that day. There was more grass around the wooden half-step to the door, but nothing had been disturbed on the outside that I could see. The door creaked at the same middle hinge as I pushed it open. It smelled musty but otherwise, the water pots remained up-side down as I had placed them on the left shelf beside the stove, the cot to the far wall was still laden with its sheets and towels now covered over to prevent dust and spider webs. The shelves with the radio, the clock and the bit of odds and ends beneath it, the double bed, still neatly made, and the kitchen table to the right, remained clean and tidy. He had not been here since. So, where did he go? I did not ask.

As I unpacked the boxes he had left inside the cabin, I found the clothes-line that I had asked for. But, it was one of those heavy nylon-coated wires with the long pulleys at each end. I put it aside. I'd have to wait until he had time to put it up. The pain and anger lay deep and heavy within my breast. I would have to wait until something happened to let it out quick or let it heal on its own... very slowly.

The weeks went by and the tension remained between us. I went about my own business. I still hung my wash on the nylon rope tied between two trees and lifted the middle with a pole I managed to find that was long enough. After another afternoon of tough laundry, I was leaning against the tree for breath, when my eyes focused on a few strands of long dark curly black hair hanging from one of the lower branches. I pulled them off. There were three strands. The person apparently got snagged in the thick lower branch. I stood running them through my fingers trying to figure out how they could have got there. His hair was short and mine was fine, long and straight. These were definitely not my hair, and not his, so whose were they? Anger rose in my chest as I began thinking, what did he do here while he left me stranded up at the Reserve? Did he bring one of his women here?

I left the strands of hair hanging from a clothes-pin. Not that he'd ever notice them! I decided not to say one blessed thing about them!

Fred had taken to leaving for long periods of time. He'd be gone all day just getting the wood, fishing or hunting for food. Even the trips to the neighbouring tourist camps became over-night affairs. He had never asked if I wanted to come. I didn't ask to accompany him. He always returned from the tourist camp smelling like beer. I hated them for giving him the drinks.

Fred was gone all night again and had returned early in the morning and without a word, he had laid down to sleep. He still slept and it was now into the afternoon. I tried to be very quiet around the cabin but decided to go out and look for some pine roots for the birch-bark basket I wanted to make.

It was a cloudy day and the smell of the earth was very strong as I wandered deep into the swampy part of the land, west of the cabin. After a while, I sat down and began to peel back thick mounds of deep moss, exposing the pine roots. I began to gently separate the long straight ones from the intermingling web. Soon my hands were quite black from coiling the roots as I removed each long strand. I had quite a few in my large apron pockets when I looked down at myself. I still wore an apron over my slacks. From the very first day I arrived here last winter, I had put on an apron. I had four and I wore each in turn. This one was quite filthy with dirt now. I had a sudden strong urge to cry as my eyes settled on the mound of my belly. At that moment, I became instantly aware of a sharp intrusion into my thoughts. I glanced around, then surveyed the area to my right more closely. I was being watched! I could feel someone watching me, but I could not see a thing. I calmly began rolling back the moss to cover the exposed roots resisting the temptation to glance around. Now, terror began to fill me as I pushed back the last chunk of moss when suddenly a fist-sized rock landed right beside me and rolled against my knee! I looked around and still I saw no one. I stood up as calmly as I could. I thought to take the rock but I could not touch what came from someone's evil hand! I began to walk away from the site, feeling the eyes glued to my back. Suddenly, in what seemed like a tremendous shot of pure animal survival instinct, I took off running at full speed, dodging to the left and right between the trees, avoiding a straight-line run. I jumped over fallen logs and crevices and stayed on the rock covered ground as much as I could. It was as I got closer to the long wood-pile that my foot landed on a large branch and I felt my ankle give. A shot of pain left me stumbling but I continued toward the cabin. Suddenly, I no longer felt the presence behind me. I slowed down as I came up behind the cabin. I was breathing hard and limping badly. I flopped down on the stump by the wood-pile beside the cabin and held the stitch of pain on my abdomen.

The door opened quickly and Fred came rushing out to me, saying, "What's the matter? What happened?"

He kept glancing around as he waited for me to answer and all I could think of to say was, "Nothing."

A furious wave of anger crossed his face and I put my head down, waiting for the onslaught.

Then he quietly said, "Come inside. I'll look at your foot."

I stood up and I could already see the swelling of my ankle beneath my sock and I gasped in pain as I gingerly hopped to the doorway, saying under my breath, "It is not my foot. It's my ankle. I twisted my ankle."

He said no more about the incident until that night as he lay stretched out beside me. "What scared you today? Your face was white as a sheet and your whole body was shaking so badly, no wonder you twisted your ankle. You're lucky you did not trip and fall. Why were you running?"

I could hear the strain in his voice. He was trying very hard not to sound angry. What could I possibly say that would make sense? That I ran and endangered the baby. That I could have fallen because I imagined someone was chasing me through the bush? That I got scared because I imagined someone was watching me when there could not possibly be any one there?

I heard myself say, "I was picking pine roots for a basket when an invisible squirrel threw a fist-sized rock at me."

I expected him to make fun of me or get angry if he thought I was making fun of his concern. Instead he said nothing for the longest time.

Then he asked, "Has the squirrel ever thrown a rock at you before?"

I answered, "No."

I didn't know where this line of questioning was going but I wasn't going to take any chances in giving him the opportunity to change this around into a metaphor that could be anybody's interpretation! I turned around and pulled the blanket around me.

My silences became longer and longer as my belly became larger. What was I going to do? I had always asked myself, now what? Now I had no answer. There was nothing I could do. I started writing my future forecasts on sheets of grocery packaging that I had cut down to notepad size. I had my treasured four pencils that I kept in my cosmetic bag where I kept all my personal things.

One day, I had just finished writing down my notes of hope and blessings that I wished for my baby on a piece of paper at the kitchen table when I heard a rattling by the door. I wondered why he was home early today. It was just after lunch and I had taken to not expecting him until late in the evening. I glanced out the window to see a big black bear sniffing around the wood-pile by the door! I barred the door with the axe that I always kept inside the cabin. It was a habit I had picked up when I was at the trap-line with my brother and sister-in-law. I waited. The bear would not go away. It hung around the door then I saw it climb to the top of the wood-pile where he decided to sit down, stretch his head and look around. He gave himself a good ol' belly scratch. After a while, he climbed back down and came toward the cabin. I couldn't see him but I knew he was just by the doorstep.

I sat down at the table and continued to write. I wrote down what

I was feeling at that moment... my loneliness, my fear, my feeling of total abandonment, and my hope for my child that we would leave this place once it was born. I could look after my own baby.

I put my head down. I must have dozed off because it was dusk when I sat up straight. Oh, my back hurt! I thought I heard something. Yes, I heard Fred coming in the boat. I heard the engine shut off at the dock and another ten minutes later, I heard him mumbling as he came up the path. I could tell he had been drinking! I jumped up and put a log in the fire, it had almost gone out.

I put the kettle on and pulled the axe out of the door-frame just in time to hear Fred exclaim, "What the heck! Get away from me, you! Shoo! Go away! Go away! Janine! Charlie!"

I pulled the door open in time to see Fred scrambling to the top of the wood-pile as the big black bear came around the corner of the cabin. I grabbed a block of wood from the pile outside the door and banged on the washtub that hung there. Bang! Bang! The bear turned, took one look at me and lumbered off into the bushes.

I could tell Fred was mighty peeved off as he stepped off the wood-pile and lunged for the door. I lit the lamp as he came in and dropped down on the bench beside the table. I was busy at the stove trying to get the fire going enough to heat the supper that I had cooked for him when I heard him swear and then he was in front of me, shoving the papers at my face. My notes! He had read them! He threw them into the stove, grabbed the stew pot and crashed it onto the floor and stomped out of the cabin. The contents of the pot splashed everywhere and the smell of it filled the room. With tearful eyes, I whirled around from the stove to see where he had gone when I slipped and fell, banging my head at the corner of the bed. The sting merged with the sudden ache in my belly before hissing darkness engulfed me.

I became aware of the smell of blood. Oh, how I hated the smell of blood! After that first time I was with Freddy when he killed the moose right outside our boat landing, I would never again forget the smell of blood! I had been soaked in blood right up to the elbows. Now, I lifted my head to see that I was on the floor of the cabin. It wasn't moose blood I was smelling, it was my own blood!

He was nowhere in the cabin. I felt along the top of my head and found a blood-congealed lump just to the side of my head.

There was the mess of the stew all over the floor. I crawled to the sink and began washing the blood off me. As I pulled myself up to reach the water-pail, I felt a kick deep inside my body. My baby! Oh, my baby! I broke down. I wailed and sobbed against the counter. I cried and cried as I had not done since I was a child. Oh, Daddy! Mom! Help me! Then I was assailed with dizzy spells followed by nausea. I crawled to the bed and curled up on top.

I gradually became aware of Freddy sponging my face with cold water on a cloth, kissing my eyes, my face, my lips, humming to me, and talking to our baby inside me. I heard promises, words of love and affection. But, I was dead. I was dead inside. I could no longer respond. Sometime in the next afternoon, or so I thought, I heard a plane land outside at our dock. Soon, I heard Gook's voice and then she was there beside me.

I found out later that Fred went to the tourist camp to radio Gook the next day to come and stay with us as I was ill with the baby. I soon got the story from Gook that I was out for at least two days from having lost so much blood. She then stated emphatically that I should not be climbing to the top of the wood-pile where I could fall down and hurt myself! She had been flitting around me, making me as comfortable as she could.

I asked her, as she was fixing my pillow, "What was his wife like?"

She stopped still for a full minute before she shoved another pillow under my head and said, "Well, she was a nice looking girl, very gentle."

She bristled under my stare and pushed the hot water bottle closer to my feet as she said, "Well, it was a few years before she married Fred when I first saw her. She was married to Fred's friend at that time. You must have known him. I believe he was from your community too. Oh, what a tragic accident that was. Poor Remy was not even a year old then..."

What did she say? Who was she talking about? But, she had gone out the door again. I waited patiently for what seemed like an eternity before she came back into the cabin again.

When she finally sat down beside me, I asked, "Gook, who was Remy's father?"

She wiped my face with a mint-smelling cloth before she responded saying softly, "Jeremiah. You remember."

Jere! That was Jere's son? Jere was the first love of my life. He was my first teenage love. Why didn't they tell me? Why didn't she tell me? Why didn't anybody tell me! Why would they?

My chest ached when it dawned on me that Remy was the other half of Jere. I remembered now that Gook said that was what the little boy called himself. Remy's baby talk. I thought it was his full name.

I slowly began to moan as another stream of tears ran down my face, in between her words of, "Now, now, don't upset yourself, he loves you, you know, he'll take care of you. He's just so upset that he might loose another wife and baby, like that first time... well, you know."

I managed to get the words out, "He hates me, Gook! He is very mean to me! He threw the pot of stew I made for him on to the floor. That's what I slipped on, Gook! I would not go climbing around on top the stupid wood-pile!"

She froze, then abruptly stood up and poured the liquid from a cup that she had been heating on top the stove. She had explained to me earlier that it was to speed up my recovery without hurting the child in me. I drank all of the contents in the cup and sank back down against the pillow in a dreadful weariness. Now, she was hugging my head to her breast and I knew she was crying in that most silent anguish that only an old woman can. I felt only the deep shudder of her chest against my head as I drifted off to sleep once more.

In what seemed like only a few minutes later, I thought I heard her giving a thundering lecture to Freddy but I was never sure whether I had been dreaming or not.

I awoke to find Freddy stroking my forehead. It was early morning and I was in his arms. I found love and warmth once again. He kissed my head, my nose, and then my lips as he stroked my belly. Then he stooped to kiss my belly too as he got up to get the fire going. It was a beautiful morning; crisp and clear. Ice had formed along the shoreline and Gook was told to be ready for the last air plane out of the tourist camp that was willing to taxi to our end of the lake.

Gook accompanied me to the outhouse and on the way back, I stopped to breathe in the fresh cold air, leaning against the wood-pile.

Then she said, "Look, there! It's Remy's cloud with the golden wig!"

It was as we stood there by the outhouse that Gook made me promise that all my mornings must be this way. If not, I must not think twice but to leave. I was shocked to hear her say that! I couldn't just leave! Not right now! It would be like admitting that I couldn't keep a relationship right; that I couldn't keep my man; that I had failed as a wife; that I couldn't keep the man I loved, happy! All the things that I had heard said in the community rushed through my mind. I wasn't ready to do that yet. Not right now. When would it be the right time? When the baby was born? What then?

As if reading my thoughts, Gook looked me right in the eyes and said, "Your love and spirit comes from deep within you. If it is not right from deep down inside you, then nothing will live outside of it. If you do not find it inside you, it will rot and fester deep inside and eventually, it will kill the spirit within you. If that happens, you will be nothing, you will care about nothing; your spirit will be broken, and your spirit will cease to exist."

I nodded. Some part of that, I could understand, the other part, I wasn't quite sure. I watched her gather the roots and herbs that she had accumulated in her short stay with us. She laid them all out in doses that I was to take until I got back to the community in late November when the ice would be thick enough to travel to a hospital for a check-up.

CHAPTER 13

There were times when Fred was assailed with tremendous fear and apprehension about the coming baby and what it might do to Janine. At other times he had felt such guilt that he hadn't made sure that she didn't get pregnant! He had figured that since she had not gotten pregnant before, then there was no reason why she should. She never told him anything!

So, in August, he had decided he would have to make sure the baby would be well taken care of when it was born. That had meant that he would have to go and see Jere's sister in Winnipeg to see if she would be willing to defray some of the money he was sending for Remy's keep into an account he wanted to set up for the baby. What else could he do? He was doing the best he could with the little money he had coming in.

In the times of total frustration, his mind would wander to the time at the spring camp by the river when he had stopped his wood cutting to watch Janine by the camp fire singeing off the feathers from the ducks. His eyes had followed her to the snow pile that she had shovelled with her snowshoes. She had dug holes, each like an oven into the snow into which she shoved a duck each. One by one she had gone across, row after row, sealing them with a wad of snow, each hole with a duck in it. He had wondered if she ever remembered anything she may have learned in the bush with her family, or whether she had just totally forgotten everything!

At that particular moment, he chuckled and said as she turned to look quizzically at him, "You forgot something, Charlie."

"What?" she said.

"You're supposed to mark each spot with a stick sticking out of it, otherwise you won't know where you buried it."

She giggled saying, "I know where I buried them. I don't need a stick to mark the spot!"

"How many do you have buried right now?"

"In total, fourteen."

When they were ready to move, he laughed hard as he watched her poking at the snow with a stick, looking for two more ducks. She had come up two ducks short! Oh, he had loved her so much at that moment, his chest hurt.

At the end of July, he stood by the shoreline thinking of her. What was he going to do? Things had remained much as before, with perhaps a bit more love and play until August when he thought to take her to Gook. There was no way he was going to see Jere's sister with her along. Jere's sister was hard enough to deal with at the best of times without having Janine and her belly to complicate things. Janine would never have believed that Remy wasn't his son! He just couldn't saddle Janine with a five year old child in the condition she was in right now. He could just imagine her thinking to herself, "So, how many of these do you have scattered around that you are still paying for?"

She had a way of speaking her mind without even opening her mouth! She could be so nasty with just one glance that would leave him shaking with rage. How dare she! But what could he respond to when she never actually said anything. Oh, she could be so frustrating!

Then there was Jere's sister. The woman was always screaming at him, saying that he was the one that had loaded her up with Remy to keep, when he was totally responsible for the boy! Yes, as he had told her, as far as he was concerned, if it wasn't for him, Jere would still be alive today! But he had never explained. There was no need. He remembered that night clearly when he and Mary decided to cozy up by the train station with the baby between them. After all, Mary had been his girlfriend long before Jere showed up. But, as always, Jere had moved in on him and then there had been Jere's baby between them. They had not even been aware that Jere was in the truck that had come to a stop across from the railway crossing when the bars came down, until they saw him running across toward them in the train's headlights. He never knew whether Jere had tripped or what. Only that he didn't make it. Then there was Mary and the baby. He had done his duty and married Mary and took the boy as his own. Then she was gone and that left the boy. He had paid Jere's sister to look after Remy and Gook was there to look after him in the summers when Jere's sister went off on vacation with her family. She had been convinced that Remy was his son and not Jere's. Well, he knew the child was Jere's son. He had not gone near Mary in that year when Remy had been conceived.

This time, he had caught Jere's sister before she left. When he saw her in Winnipeg, they argued and he had won the battle with the promise that he would take Remy off her hands forever and look after him when he was married to Janine. He decided not to tell her that there was a baby on the way too.

He had been quite happy when he left their apartment and headed for downtown Winnipeg. Who would have thought, but who would come yelling and screaming at him from one of the hotel bars, but Big Al, Karen's husband! Oh, he was in one big snot of a temper! He hadn't even quite made out what the problem was before he felt the blow coming and just ducked enough that it missed his face but the big fist landed squarely on the side of his head. He went down spinning and fell flat on his back, and heard a sharp crack as his head hit the sidewalk pavement. Bright stars spun around inside his eyes. Instinctively anticipating a kick across his middle, he quickly rolled away, kicking sideways as hard as he could. Sure enough, there was contact with one of the big man's legs and the man came down hard, right on the edge of a cement step leading to the hotel bar that he had just emerged from. People came running as Fred pushed himself to his feet and stood there swaying as he stooped to check the guy with the pool of blood beside his head. The police and ambulance came. At the police station, he found out that the guy was now in the hospital. Well, to make a long story short, he spent time in jail until a witness verified that he had not even fought back at all and that the big man had tripped. Fight back, heck! Nothing could have stopped Big Al. He would have tried to fight back all he wanted but he was just lucky he was able to trip him. He knew for sure that Big Al would have beat him to a pulp if he had got his hands on him.

When he was finally released from jail, he headed straight to Armstrong and picked up the supplies that he needed and flew them to the trapper's shack and from there, made straight to the Reserve. He had been so relieved that she was still there. But in all truth, she may have been there in body only because there was this distance that she had put between him and her and try as he might, there was one huge cement wall between them now and he couldn't do a darned thing about it! There was no way she would believe anything he said, so he didn't bother trying to explain. What did she want from him anyway? What did she want?

There was another thing that bothered him immensely. The tourist guide Jason, was always hanging around the site when he wasn't home! He had seen the man several times and before he could get out to check, there was no one in sight. Of course when he asked him why he didn't hang around until he got back, Jason didn't know what he was talking about, huh!

Another time, he had come in roaring full speed on his twenty-five Johnson motor only to find Jason waiting inside the cabin. Jason's excuse was that he had seen him in a canoe coming into the landing, so he had come across only to find out that he wasn't home. So, who the heck was in the canoe? He had the boat and the canoe was turned over at the boat landing! Janine had just looked at him with one of her blank expressions as if she didn't know what was going on!

Then there was the time when a lightning storm hit very badly and the wind was threatening to knock the tree down in front of the cabin at any moment. He had glanced out in time to see what he was certain was the head and shoulders of a man behind the wood-pile. By the time he had got out there, there was no one in sight.

It was around that time several days later when he came across the boot print beside his canoe that had made him dash up to the cabin in such a hurry he did not see the bear until he nearly stumbled upon it by the door! Oh, man, now that had got him scrambling up the wood-pile so fast, he was embarrassed that Janine had saved him from the black bear. Or so, she thought.

That was when... oh, well. He hated to think of that time. He had stopped trying to rationalize what was possessing him to treat her like that. Gook had been so angry she had actually slapped him across the face with her medicine bag. Then he saw how immediately sorry she was for big welts of tears had sprung into her eyes. He had pulled her into his arms. Oh, how sorry he was for the stupid things he had done in his life! There was only one other single human being in his entire life that he would never ever hurt for absolutely any reason and that was his Gook! To be the cause of those tears that sprang in her eyes, had wrenched his soul. But God! How he loved the people he seemed to be hurting the most!

He was just reacting to situations now. He felt that he was absolutely no longer in control of anything. He was just waiting to see what would happen next and the result was never his doing at all! The things that were happening... there was just nothing he could do about things he had absolutely no control over!

He wished Janine would talk to him, tell him who had been and was still visiting her when he was away working, getting wood, checking his traps, fishing or hunting for food! But, no, she said nothing at all. She just looked at him with those bewildered, questioning looks, or worse still and more often of late, the silent accusations, the snide comment looks, and her actions and expressions all condemning him, without her ever having to open her mouth! If he ever dared to mention the strange foot prints or the man he saw at times around the cabin, she just looked at him with those blank hurt stares and turned her head away without comment.

In her own way, she was always telling him that he was nuts and that she was innocent of all accusations and how dare he question her! What was he to think then?

So, without a word to Janine, he helped Jason with the construction of a new ice house at the tourist camp. She wouldn't care anyway, he thought. It was one more thing not to argue over because he promised her that he'd build a wood-shed, instead there he was building an ice-shed at the tourist camp. Days came and went and she got bigger and bigger. Would she leave when the baby was born? That was what she had written on the pieces of paper. Oh, how much that had hurt him! But then, maybe the baby wasn't even his anyway! After all, who was this guy that was hanging around the camp that he had yet to catch. But when he did, he had no doubt what he would do with him come snow or high water!

Ha, ha, ha! I am thoroughly enjoying this! Why didn't I think of this before? Well, perhaps it had been too long since I walked among the people. As you can see, I am very, very good at this. Do you want to see how quickly a man can go crazy?

There were times during the day that Fred would try to trick Jason into confessing he had been to the trapper's shack when Fred wasn't in. Instead, he got many accounts of the times when Jason would drive down there only to find that Fred's boat and motor was gone from the dock, when he had expected the canoe to be gone, as it would be if that had been Fred in the canoe that Jason had seen. But, there was never any trace of anything, or any glimpse of anyone other than those on the lake. Fred felt that after all the time he had spent with Jason, that if he was any judge of character, he knew now that Jason could not be the man around the cabin. So, who was it then? No one saw anything! That was what was making him so furious. Well, he had come to the end. This had to stop and he was going to make sure that this did not go on to another year.

He could almost pin-point the moment when things began to get screwy and that was around the time Janine came to the trap-line. Was it someone who was trying to keep her out? Who? Who could it be? He doubted it was someone from the community, otherwise people would know. Someone would know if one of the guys was up to no good! He'd know if someone had been gone when he got back. But, no. Everyone was always where they were supposed to be and nothing seemed unusual when he got back. After that first time when he had nearly stepped into one of the connibear traps, he had been very careful and watchful. He found the trap right below the tree where he had the whole bunch hanging. He knew she hadn't done it. There was no way Charlie would be able to pull and set a large trap like that. Why would she do such a thing like that anyway? They had been quite happy then.

Who then, was hanging around the trap-line? Maybe it was a parasite who had attached himself to her, following her from wherever she had been. Thunder Bay? Would someone be following her from there? He doubted that any city person would be able to allude him in his own territory! He discounted the idea that anyone from the city could be following her and certainly no one from the community.

He listened to the snap and crackle of the last flare of birch logs that he had thrown into the wood-stove and carefully placed his arm around Janine's middle, cradling the baby within her belly in the flickering lights from the stove. His baby. He would protect his wife and little baby with his life. No one would take them away from him! They were his. They were home with him, safe and sound.

CHAPTER *14*

It was around the second week of October and I stood outside feeling slightly exasperated. Fred had gone off early. It was around mid-morning when Jason stopped to say goodbye. He was going on the last plane out from the tourist camp and waited around for about half an hour but Fred didn't come home. I put the two boxes of food that Jason brought inside the cabin. The food had been left by the last tourists in the cabins. Jason said he had finished boarding all the buildings and locked everything up for the winter. Then he was gone, wishing me luck with the baby. It was now late afternoon; cold, and overcast and still no sign of Fred.

We had snow many times in the last three weeks but it always melted the next day. But winter would soon be here and the clothesline was still not up and he had not put the boat and canoe away yet either! I hoped that the washed clothes would have softened somewhat in the breeze before they froze into stiff boards last night. And the bit of snow this morning left them soaking wet again! I wished he had put up the new clothesline to make room for my new wash today but he just never seemed to have the time. The little nylon line could only hold up a few sheets at a time and I had much more to do at one go now because I could not wash two or three loads a week as I had done before.

I was also still smarting from the incident yesterday. After I had hung up the washing, I saw that the long pole I used to prop up the line to keep the clothes off the ground was leaning against the green wood log pile. As I tugged, I found that it was pinned at the top by a long pine log. I pulled hard and suddenly, in a thundering roar, the top logs cascaded down the pile! I barely got out of the way as one log swung off the pile and landed end first right where I had been standing. Quite shaken, I went in for a cup of tea, before I picked up the pole again. Why had he done that? He would have had no need to move the logs since he had not cut any firewood in about a week. When he got back, he had made no comment as I watched him pile the logs back up into a neat pile.

I was quite skinny, thinner than I had ever been which made my belly larger than it perhaps would have appeared. Anyway, I just didn't have the energy these days. It was at this moment that Fred came around the corner of the cabin. He looked furious about something. I turned from the clothesline and took two blocks of dry wood into the cabin. He stood aside as I went in. I took a seat at the table and waited. He stopped beside me and pulled out my blue shirt from under his coat. I looked at the shirt. It was my favourite one with flowers embroidered around the collar. I wondered where it had gone to. I was searching for it everywhere at the last washing. When was that? Four days ago? Jason had laughed at me when I asked him what day it was. Although I had a calendar hanging on the wall, if I did not make a diligent effort to mark off each day, I soon lost track which day it was, because it basically did not matter one bit which day it was out here.

Suddenly Fred was barking at me, "Look at this. Isn't this the shirt I bought you?"

I looked up at him and simply said, "Yes, it is the one you bought for me at Savant Lake."

He took a big breath and threw it on the table in front of me as he gritted out each syllable between his teeth, "I found it on top the last wood-pile deep in the bush. How did it get there?"

I looked at the shirt thinking, how on earth would it get there unless he was just making this up just to get mad at me for something.

He was still standing there glaring at me so what was I supposed to say? I just shrugged and said, "I don't know."

He still had not moved and I waited.

Finally he said, "He was here again wasn't he?"

I wondered who he was talking about. I wouldn't consider Jason's visit to see Fred an "again."

I looked at him and simply replied, "No one has ever been here, except Jason. He came to say goodbye to you this morning just before lunch-time. He brought two boxes of left over food, right there beside the door, and to tell you that he had boarded up the tourist camp and the key was where he usually left it in case the boss ever wants it. He was leaving on the last plane out which must have been the one I heard taking off around mid-afternoon. And he wished us luck with the baby. He waited for a little while for you before he left. But, that was all."

That was the longest string of words I had uttered in many, many, months. He took one exasperated look around at the cabin and then focussed his attention on me for one full minute before he stomped out of the cabin. I heard his footsteps recede. I had no idea when he would return. I really didn't care anymore.

After I'd had a cup of tea, I went back outside and looked up at the pine tree. Then with new determination, I dug out the box from under the table and pulled out the huge roll of nylon covered wire clothes-line with the two pulleys and hauled them outside. I lugged one end of the coil to my shoulder and up the wood-pile and shoved my foot on top the first branch of the tall pine tree. I climbed that tree quite high until I was sure that no amount of slack would drag the clothes down. Then I set about wrapping the wire around the tree and got the pulley positioned right. It was as I tugged the bottom wire through the pulley that my foot slipped off the lower branch. I was slammed against the tree so hard I lost my breath. I gasped and hung on tight with both hands to the branch until the pain receded from my side.

Suddenly, there was Freddy screaming his head off at the bottom of the tree! Oh, man, I knew I was in trouble. I climbed down very slowly and carefully. Not because I was afraid to fall, but because there were now continuous stabs of pain on my left side.

I stepped down to the ground with Fred still stomping around yelling that I was deliberately trying to kill his baby. What?

It registered in my brain what he was yelling about and I reacted with my own, now strangely unfamiliar voice yelling, "What did you say?

That I am trying to kill our baby? Do you honestly believe that I would intentionally hurt someone growing inside me? It is you who is trying to kill us! Me and the baby! You don't want us, do you? Why don't you just kill us right now instead of torturing me to death!"

I could have said a lot more. I had stored enough awful things in my head to keep my mouth going for a long time. But, then, he was nowhere around. As always, he had just whirled around and left. Who knows where he goes and I didn't much care at that point. He may have built another trapper's shack with his other women housed in it for all I knew!

On a sudden impulse, I hobbled down to the lake and saw that his boat was still pulled up on shore. I turned the canoe over and pushed it out into the water. Grabbing a paddle, I stepped in and pushed the canoe off. I started paddling out into the open steel-grey lake. Perhaps a bit of paddling would calm my anger. The pain in my side had receded to a dull ache. I heard the motor starting behind me and then there was Fred coming at me full speed. I dropped my paddle as I grabbed the sides of the canoe to steady myself as the waves crashed against the side of the canoe!

So close did he come that I screamed at him, "You! You stinking rotten muskrat! You flea-bitten mangy dog!"

He lunged forward and grabbed my arm, yelling, "Get into the boat right now! The canoe is sinking!"

I stopped and looked down and low and behold, the canoe had a good two inches of water in it! With his old pair of rubber boots on my feet, I hadn't noticed. I shut up and got into the boat and we towed the water-laden canoe to shore without another word between us.

It was as I was heading up the path that I heard him grumble under his breath as he pulled the half-filled canoe to shore, saying, "Why the heck she did this, I'll never know!"

I stomped into the cabin thinking, yes, blame me. Always blame me. Half the time, I haven't a clue what he blames me about or gets so mad about! That must have been quite a big hole in the canoe for it to have filled up like that.

I took a swig of Gook's medicine and lay down on the bed and waited.

I awoke to find that I was still in the same position on the bed and it was very quiet with only the sound of the flickering fire in the wood-stove. I got up and went to the window. There was full moonlight and I noticed that all the clothes were on the new clothesline! I turned to see Freddy sprawled out in all his clothes on the spare bunk he had set up beside the wood-stove. I went to him, knelt down beside the bunk and slowly brushed back the hair from his forehead. I was so totally emotionally exhausted from the tension between us and I wanted so desperately just to hold him and concentrate only on him and to love him freely and openly.

His eyes flickered open and I kissed his lips and whispered, "I love you Freddy. Thank you for the clothesline."

He didn't say a thing but looked at me for a full minute. I grew uncomfortable and pulled away. I got into the bed with the goose-down-filled comforter that we had filled from our spring hunting and camping session last spring. He did not join me in bed. I had tried to reach out but I was now kicking myself for trying. He may as well have pushed me away. He didn't want me. I lay alone in the warm comfort of the feathers that we had so much fun picking together. I felt such an intense pain across my chest, I could have cried and sobbed for a whole week. But, I lay dry-eyed and looked into the blackness of the night.

Things went relatively well for the rest of the month. I never did find out what caused the hole in the canvas canoe other than that Fred had to patch an inch and a half gash on its bottom. After my outburst in the canoe, I still felt shame at what I had called him but I could find no way to apologize. I could never take back what I had said. So, at times it revisited me.

One instance was on an evening when I heard Fred coming in on the boat, and I went down to see him by the cleaning lean-to that he had built where he either cleaned fish or skinned pelts of the smaller animals. This time, he had a muskrat on the table. He smiled as I approached.

Then casting a side glance at me, a grin travelled across his face and he said, "Oh, it's just a stinking rotten muskrat!"

I reacted like he had just slapped me in the face. He was throwing my words back in my face! The pain spread across my chest and I blinked back the tears as I veered away and headed to the shoreline.

I heard him coming after me but then he stopped and I felt him standing there, as though wondering what to do. I took a deep breath and looked at the sky. I must not cry. I turned and saw that he was back at the lean-to. I walked back to the cabin and set the teapot on the stove. Come to think of it, I never did find out what my blue shirt had been doing at the wood-pile either. But, I was very careful not to disturb this new tentative openness that had developed between us and I really hoped nothing else would happen.

As the snowstorms came, quietness descended. The out-board motor was now housed in the corner under my kitchen table. There was enough wood piled under layers of canvas just outside the door. There was no need for the power-saw. What hunting he did, was along the shoreline or in the bay about a mile from the cabin. Most of the time, he was in the woods for we were at a point of land and he could travel from one side to the other in half a day. He knew where the moose would be but he had to wait until it was cold enough to freeze the meat.

We had some funny moments and some light-hearted fun, but nothing of the happiness we felt when we first came here. I realized it was partly to do with my big belly and the cramps that suddenly assailed me at times, but on the whole, it was nice. I had a new sense of safety and comfort with the onset of the snow because, as I figured it, I had nothing to fear of things that did not make any tracks in the snow. But, I still dreaded the coming Christmas season and wondered what would happen then.

I had the strong urge at times to run to my note-making pads to write down what I'd like to see happen. But, there was one thing that Fred had said last week that got me to thinking. It was the only mention to the notes that he had found on the table that evening when the bear had kept me indoors.

I was sharpening a pencil to sketch the outdoor evening scene when Freddy had paused over me and said, "You jinx the things you wish for when you write them down you know?"

Then, he went out with the water-pail.

I rolled the pencil between my fingers thinking that maybe he was right. Did any of the things I wrote down ever come true? No. I cannot honestly say that they ever had. I must destroy all my well-wishing notes about the baby! I scrambled around to all the nooks and crannies and shoved every page into the stove before I heard his footsteps coming up the path.

From that time on, I sketched the scenes outdoors, the clouds with the golden wigs, the trees, the islands and the scenes inside the cabin. Most of the time, I sketched Fred at work; stretching animal hides, hauling wood, cutting wood, splitting wood, hauling water and building a cradle that looked much like a huge snow-shoe without the front or bottom. It was a meshed-in structure, with all the sides and bottom laced with woven rawhide. I sewed in a beadwork pattern of flowers on leather at the head and foot piece. We worked on this cradle together from beginning to end. It was the one thing we had worked on together. We had made it together and it was really quite beautiful.

Our preparation for our baby was finished by the end of the third week of December. We laid the cradle down on the bunk beside the stove. I had made it clear that I was not interested in going into the community for the Christmas holidays. Freddy, on the other hand was insistent that he should get us Christmas presents and some grocery treats. I was partial to agreeing since I had developed such an insatiable taste for peanut butter. I had made him promise to bring back at least a dozen jars or cans for me. He needed to replace some connibear traps and we needed some more rice, flour, baking powder, oats, lard and perhaps some face cream for my stretched belly. My face felt so dry at times that I may have looked as bad as I felt. I was still very much concerned at my weight-loss when I should have been gaining weight, or so I imagined a pregnant woman should. I mean, what did I know?

And then there was the other thing I really longed for. I had noticed some wolf tracks by the farthest wood-pile the last time I went for a walk. I mentioned them to Fred and added, "If we had a dog, it would bark and chase it away."

He had been laying down with his hands behind his head as he always did, and now he came up on one elbow and looked at me, "You want a dog? Why didn't you say so."

Then he came and knelt down beside me and cupped my face in his hands and added, "And, I promise I will not bring home a flea-bitten mangy one."

I recognized the words and knew the reference but his gentle eyes held mine and his hands were firm around my face, and this time I understood. I was forgiven. My tears flowed down my cheeks and his thumbs wiped them aside. He held me still and lightly kissed me and as he did lately, he also bent down and kissed my belly.

Chapter 15

He left on the twenty-third of December and the days went by. Christmas came and went. And then, New Year's Day was gone and I knew he had goofed up once again. He had good intentions but things easily distracted him and they would have to run their course before he'd remember what he was supposed to have done or where he was supposed to have been. So, he'd just have to immediately concentrate on what he was supposed to be doing and where he was supposed to be going, or I was in big trouble!

One sunset after another, the days came and went. I had my rabbit snares to keep me going. I regularly caught one rabbit a day. If I did not feel like having a rabbit for supper, I always had a partridge in the box on top the roof.

The other things that got on my nerves, were the martins! Man, you couldn't hide anything from those guys. And there was the lady! There was Josiah, Peter, Terry, the rascal Oscar Martin and the lady Lucy. I absolutely had no liking whatsoever for Oscar! He was the most vindictive, meanest martin I had ever come across in my entire life! I would have clamped a trap around that old rascal with my own bare hands if it wasn't for the thought of catching Lucy instead. Oh, she was a sweet girl, that Lucy! Oh, well, never mind, that old raven was back at my fish freezer box again! Between the ravens, martins, and the blue jays, I wondered if I still had some fish left to eat!

I had just made some jam from some frozen blueberries that we had in the box on the roof when I felt the first searing pain. Chalking it down to perhaps some gas pain, I endured the regular cramps on into the evening. It was now the eleventh of January and I still had another three weeks to go before the baby was due. What were these pains? I was still alone. It was then that I realized that with all my worrying and waiting for Fred, I had not felt the baby move in a long time! When was the last time I felt the baby move? Last week? No, it was four, five days ago?

I experienced the gut-wrenching spasms of intense sharp pains diminishing into an acute ache before my belly was assailed into another searing pain. I had endured the cramps at regular intervals all through the night and now it was the twelfth of January. What was I to do? I was terrified of having the baby all alone! I had told him not to leave me alone for no more than three days this time! No more than three days, I had begged him! What if something went wrong, please do not leave me for no more than three days, please! I begged him. He had been gone now, for two and a half weeks!

As the pains continued at regular intervals, I knew I was in trouble. I didn't know what to do. I did not know a thing about babies! I was supposed to go to the Sioux Lookout hospital at the end of January to wait until the baby came. That was the plan. Now, what was I to do? I cursed Fred and swore that I would never, never ever forgive him for this! In final desperation, I began to pack some things into a packsack. Into the packsack went four baby blankets still in the packages, baby socks, several baby gowns, a bottle, matches, baby diapers, raisins, a can of milk, a knife and a chunk of bannock. Next went my personal cosmetic bag and then, I could not think of any think else. I did not know what I'd need!

I tied a flannel blanket around my middle and folded a quilt over the seat of the old snow machine. I prayed to God that it would get me through the whole seventy miles back to the community. Freddy got so fed up with this old machine stalling that he had finally bargained for the newer machine that he took with him. I had only used it once to get some wood. It still ran but it had a tendency to stall after a while and it would stay that way for several weeks before it would start again after Fred took it apart for the zillionth time.

"Oh, Freddy!" I was screaming in my head, "Why are you doing this to me? You couldn't have just left me alone like this for no reason.

Why? What's happened? Has something happened to you Fred? Are you still alive? What's happened? You wouldn't just leave me like this, would you? Would you?"

No amount of questions halted the spasms of pain that ripped through my back and across my belly. I only knew that labour was supposed to take a long time. I hoped to goodness, there was enough time to make it back to the village.

I started the old machine on a prayer after I had put the lights and the stove out in the cabin. I thought of leaving a note for Freddy, but after that episode about the notes, I decided to forget about the idea. I had to have a deeper faith that things would be alright and we would be all together again, Freddy, baby and me.

The old machine started like clock work. I estimated the time to be about eight o'clock in the evening. My watch had long ago died and since we had no need for a clock, I had no idea of the exact time when I left the cabin. I hoped and prayed that I would meet Fred somewhere along the winter trail as I pressed the throttle and the machine sped across the lake. Without slowing down, I roared over the creek and into the dense swamp bush, up and down the hills, through the Devil's Gorge jump of over ten feet across, at full speed with only two skinny pine poles bridging the ten-foot deep gorge. I didn't even hold a breath. I'd been through there before. My only thought was to line up the machine, close my eyes, hold my breath and press the throttle at full speed. Soon, I was out into clear bright moonlight on Whitewater Lake. The machine roared at a constant rhythm beneath me as another cramp seized me across the middle. I moaned as I hit a deep snow-drift and then I was out onto hard packed snow. I crossed the lake and was eventually at the marsh area right of Best Island. It was somewhere in the middle of the centre pond when I suddenly hit a rather mean snow-drift. It threw me such a sharp jerk to the right that the pain shot like a huge boulder right through my belly straight out of my back! The machine continued on at full speed as I gasped to catch my breath and steady myself from the pain.

My mind screamed, "I do not want to have a baby in the middle of nowhere on the ice!" I knew that there was no one around at all on this lake at this time of the year. My hands clamped on to the speed clutch at break-neck speed, right across the island and straight on to the narrows. I eased off a bit as the machine climbed up the bank and into the portage. Applying more speed as I came out the other end of the portage, another spasm invaded my abdomen. I clamped my hands around the throttle at full speed across the short bay and into another portage sending sheets of snow spraying at each snowdrift and I came out careening into a solid snow-cap that sent me sailing back on to the path. I went on at full speed as another pain doubled me over.

It was another half hour before I emerged at Loon Narrows. I remembered the place from my childhood. Oh, Dad, help me! Father, help me! I moaned out loud and wailed, cried,and screamed as I barrelled through the narrows and out into the wide open frost-hazed Smoothrock Lake. Another sweat-drenching pain enveloped me as I passed through the two islands. I was still a long way to the other end where the other portage was. It was somewhere in the middle of the lake when the machine first started to sputter.

I screamed out loud at it, "Oh, no! No, No! Please don't do this to me!" There was absolutely no other soul around for the next thirty miles!

"No!" But, the machine stopped dead.

I stood leaning over the handle bars as another sweat-drenching pain passed over me. I couldn't stop now! I had to keep going! I pulled once just as another pain shot across my middle and I screamed out load. I tried to time the next pull when I felt the pain receding. In this way, I pulled and pulled to get the machine started. Finally the machine sputtered to life and I managed to go very slowly for another mile or so. On and on I went. Stop and go, until I managed to cross the portage out of Smoothrock Lake and into the channel and then gradually into the small lakes that led into the last lake before the last long portage into the community.

After that last stop, it was a long three mile portage to the community. It was where I expected Fred to be. It was where my mother was. I could see the early morning tint the eastern horizon as I managed to get the machine going again after about the fourteenth pull on the engine. What seemed to be the hardest job of all was the pulling! I'd pull the string on the engine to get it going and each pull sent a sharp pain across my huge belly. Eventually, each pull meant a sharp groan as the pain intensified across my middle and lower back. I maneuvered the machine across the dense bush and was finally outside the last portage when the machine stopped again. Except this time, at my last pull of the snow machine when I got the machine going again, I felt a gush of something breaking beneath me. I looked down at my feet and saw the snow coloured with red. If my water broke, why was it red? Was it supposed to be red? Why would they call it water if it was red? There had been no hide nor hair of wolves throughout my whole crazy night of travel, otherwise, at this point, I would have been scared out of my wits! I had but three miles to go at the least. My water had broke, but the machine was going again, and there was no sign of wolves... for the time being. I eased off on the throttle as I crept slowly up the hill and into the bushes, but when the pain seized me again with a ferocious force this time, I involuntarily clamped on the throttle at full speed through the bush road's left and right turns, up and down the gulleys and swamp log trails. I'm sure I must have came shooting out of the portage trail so fast that it caught the attention of the old man who lived in the last cabin of the community.

As I later heard it, the old man had apparently been bringing his morning firewood into his cabin when he heard the snow machine come to a sudden stop in the bushes by the graveyard. The old man waited a while before he decided to take his toboggan to go and check. As he'd always said, a machine running out of gas was always appreciative of someone showing up with gas on his sleigh. Only this time, he found a woman, drenched in blood, straining to have a baby that wasn't coming out.

Mother came with me to the hospital in Sioux Lookout. I felt the bandages at my belly where they had taken out my dead baby. Sometime later in the day, I awoke to find Freddy sitting beside me.

I heard my voice screaming, "Get out! Get out!"

I was told that I was lucky to be alive and that my husband had been sitting there all day waiting to see me. I let the nurses know that I did not have a husband and they were not to let anyone else besides my mother to come near me until I was able to leave the hospital. I grieved for my baby and I was extremely angry the whole time I spent at the hospital. On top of that, an infection had set in and I was set in for another week or so at the hospital. And so they had buried the baby without me. If I had seen him at that time, I would have punched Freddy from here to kingdom come, along with whatever other woman he had been with! I blamed everyone for the hell I had just gone through! Why hadn't someone come to check up on me when I was in the bush? I did a lot of screaming and crying at that hospital in those several weeks. The unfortunate thing was that it was all done silently inside my head.

When I finally arrived back at the village, I got the news when I stopped by the post office on the way to my mother's place. The postman informed me that our good friend Linda had a fatal car accident sometime after the New Year. In my mind, somehow, there was no separation between the pain I felt with the loss of my baby, Linda and Freddy. They all rolled into one horrible gigantic pain that invaded every space in my heart, mind and soul.

I lay on the single cot beside the window in my mother's cabin and rolled myself into a ball. And for the very first time, I discovered unreasonable fear. Every footstep coming to the door sent my heart racing against my ribs. I was terrified that Fred would show up yelling and screaming that I had killed our baby. And I couldn't cry. I had not cried at all. The days came and went. The Groundhogs kept me well fed or else they would not leave me alone until I ate. I soon became stronger. About a week later, we heard an airplane land. Then we heard a snow machine coming toward the cabin. My heart raced through me again as I backed up against the wall by the bed in fear.

I heard voices and then the Groundhogs burst in yelling, "Someone's come to see you, Janine!"

Oh, no! I grabbed my jacket, but then there was Gook! She made a bee-line across the floor to me. She hugged and kissed me, holding me for the longest time as she shed silent tears. At one point, I lifted my head to see my mother by the table watching us. I could not understand the look that crossed her face until I realized that perhaps she wished she could do that too; hug people, hug me I mean. It most likely never occurred to her to do that... maybe wondering if she could, if she tried.

Gook stayed for several days, and then after a long conversation with Mother, we decided on what I should do. With the help of the Groundhogs, armed with an axe and a hammer, we headed to the other side of the community to Fred's cabin. The boys had the padlock and hinges off the door in no time and we entered. The snow machine was still there in the middle of the floor. Fred always brought his snow machine inside when he was going on the train. I guessed he had not been back since. My suitcases were where I had left them. Everything that went to the trap-line was packed in wooden crates and paper boxes. All my town clothes were still in the suitcases. I was never one to leave any of my things scattered around, but I watched Gook shove one of my sweaters into the suitcase.

I stood and looked around. For the first time, I felt the urge to cry.

Gook said behind me, "Let it all go, Channie. Let it go. Leave it all here within these cabin walls. Logs are very good at that you know, they take out the pain and sorrow from you. They absorb it all. Leave it all with them. If you take any of the bad feelings with you, they will fester within you like a huge sore. Let them all go. Leave the hurt and ugliness within these walls. They will take it all from you and it won't hurt you again... so bad."

I took a deep breath and walked out the door. The boys nailed the hinges and padlock back on the door and we walked to the train station. We got on the train with no more than a wave from Mother and the Groundhogs.

We were halfway to Sioux Lookout when Gook said, "I want to tell you that I put some money in the suitcase when I put the sweater in. It is not mine so don't feel bad. Fred has always sent me money over the years.

That was the only way I knew where he was. From the time his mother died, he decided that he would take care of me. He never told me to keep it for him, he just sent me the money. Now, what am I going to do with the money? I am an old woman, I don't need the money. I have enough to live on on my own. Remy has his own money, so, what you find in the suitcase is yours. It is yours. Don't argue with me, just take it and use it to get started again."

I looked out the window and said nothing. Some part of me had died sometime last month. My problem was not knowing which part. How could I even begin to heal myself if I wasn't quite certain where the exact spot of injury lay. I just seemed to hurt all over! I mean, I was in agonizing pain, mentally and spiritually, although the physical pain may have been gone. But then, in my sleep, you couldn't tell that to my body either. I still woke up in the middle of the night dreaming that the baby was kicking... oh, that tore me apart! It was at those times when I stared into the darkness until the sun came up.

I felt Gook take my hand and we sat like that until the train rolled into Sioux Lookout. She was going on to Winnipeg to see a cousin and it was where she expected to find Fred. I never knew they had other relatives there. I gave her a hug and left the train at Sioux Lookout. When I got to the hotel room, I began to unpack for a hot bath when I found the bag. I unrolled the sweater and what I thought to be perhaps around fifty dollars, came to one thousand and twenty-five dollars! It was in money orders, one hundred dollar bills, fifty dollar bills and fives. I was totally shocked! Tears came gushing out in a torrent of emotion. I finally released the tears that I had kept bottled up for so long.

CHAPTER 16

I took my time finding a job in Thunder Bay. I mostly sat in a motel for about four days looking at myself in the dresser mirror. It had occurred to me that I no longer knew the person sitting before me. I had been through so much, and all of that had been on my own. I had no one to share those experiences with. In the whole time I had been away, I had not seen myself in a mirror or had anyone to balance my thoughts and feelings with. I mean someone with whom to talk with who would set my sights straight and help me find a balanced perspective, "an even-keeled point of view" as Linda would have described it. Oh, how I missed her! I think that maybe I had sunk too far to one side, long ago.

A week later when I thought I found some semblance of myself, I got up and went hunting for a furnished apartment. About three days later, I found a nice cozy little place close to downtown Port Arthur. Then I got a job a short time after that at the Indian Affairs Counselling Unit and began rebuilding my life, slowly, one day at a time.

About eight months later, Nisha suddenly walked into the office and stood leaning against the counter, looking at me with a slight smile on his face. He had come to pick me up for lunch he said. I looked at him, at a total loss for what to say. Without a word, I got up and we went for lunch at a restaurant downstairs at Eaton's. I wasn't saying much, so he did all the talking. Then before I realized it, he had me laughing with his endless tales of comical situations. We sat in the shade of the trees outside the office before I went back in. I smiled upon remembering that he replied, "Nisha-bego," to my question as to why he had come into town.

I've got her now! She's mine! You see, I took care of Fred. I took

that baby too. I want her all to myself. All to myself. All to myself.
All to myself... Wait, I feel the sense of someone. Someone knows
me. I feel him searching for me. I must see who it is. Distract.
That's it!

As the days went by, Nisha showed up at lunch-time at least three times a week. He had found a job at a warehouse somewhere. He was still driving that truck that had broke down on him when I first met him. It was a warm evening in October when we walked up to Hillcrest Park. It was there that he first put his arm around me. Then quite unexpectedly, he leaned over and kissed me. I, like an old partridge, froze and didn't move. I knew then that this was not going to go anywhere. I pushed him back and explained that I was not ready for another relationship and that all he could ever hope from me was just a friend. He looked quite shocked as if that was the last thing in the world he expected to hear. He said nothing. He walked me home. We chatted along the way as if I had not said anything. What was he doing, pretending that it never happened? I said nothing about it either.

Then he disappeared. I never saw him again as Christmas neared. I went to work and came home, and stayed home on the weekends. I never went anywhere, or felt the need to.

One evening in January, I walked by my living-room window and saw a man leaning against the lamp post across the street. I pulled the curtain shut and glanced out once more before it closed, but he was gone. I had no idea who it could have been. It now occurred to me it was mostly in the evenings when I came home, that a man would materialize somewhere along the street, but each time I tried to take a closer look he was gone. I never thought that maybe he could have any thing to do with me, until now! Did he? I always thought it was just someone out for a walk or something. Now it got me to thinking that maybe it was as if he waited until I got home and then left. Could it be Fred? I couldn't be certain because he always stood in the shadows or had a big parka on with the hood pulled low.

I was coming home one evening and it was about the fifth time that I saw him there. This time he had a short snowsuit jacket on. I turned around at the door just in time to see him move into the light and I recognized him. It was Freddy! Shock and anger shot through me. How dare he! Furious, I ran toward him as fast as I could. I was going to make sure he never dared hang around my door again! I ran flat out right across the street, yelling his name, just as he started to turn. He stopped when he saw me coming and waited. Just when I was within arm's length, he grabbed me and pulled me into his arms! I was just catching my breath and starting to push myself away when he crushed me to his chest and I couldn't move. At that moment, I saw a truck slow down beside my apartment and then the screech of tires as it sped away down the street. It was Nisha! What was he doing here? I had thought he had gone out of town again. But, maybe it wasn't him. Could have been another truck. I started hitting Fred on the chest until he released me and shoved me away.

I stood back gasping, "Go away! Don't you ever touch me again. Stay out of my life!"

He threw his head back and laughed, a menacing, idiotic laugh, I thought. His face was gaunt, dark, lined and badly in need of a shave. Then he turned and quickly walked away. I ran blindly back to my apartment. Why was he doing this to me? How long had he been stalking me? Had he gone mad? He didn't sound sane. A shudder went up my back.

Towards the end of January, my phone rang. It was the postmaster from my home community. My mother was sick and was asking me to come home. I put the phone down and cried bitterly for about an hour before I started packing. I had to go back. I would call work from there. I hoped Mother wasn't seriously ill. I hated the thought of having to give up this place and my own sense of security, or whatever was left of it. I would pay one extra month so that I wouldn't lose the place, but I was going to lose my job. I'd had only temporary jobs that lasted for three months or six months at the most. Others had been extended for a few months more. At the last competition, this was the most steady job I had so far. I did not want to lose it now.

I caught a bus to Nakina and took the evening train west. I got off the train at eleven o'clock amongst the hissing steam. I could hardly see the little step that the conductor placed on the ice-covered gravel beside the railway tracks. His hand on my arm kept me balanced as I stepped off the train and still quite distracted with worry, I automatically nodded to him.

"Thank you... very much sir, and good night."

There was an unmistakable pause of a few seconds before he reacted, "And good night to you too, Miss."

The community people getting on, stood aside as I stepped off and waited as I got my suitcase that the other conductor was handing down to the one beside me. I took my suitcase and this time, I whispered thank-you, as I turned and stepped around the people.

I made my way along the path that ran parallel to the railway tracks and across the creek toward Mother's place. The train was gone and the path was deserted. All I heard was the snow crunching under my feet. Oh, my! Was it ever cold here! I had no sooner gone half way when I heard footsteps coming at a run behind me. I paused and put my suitcase down thinking that whoever was coming up behind me in such a hurry could very well go around me. It was Ron. He came to a stop beside me and after a brief silence, he took my suitcase. I walked ahead and he followed behind me without a word until we got to the top of the hill where I stopped and turned around. He put the suitcase down and faced me. The moon was full and I saw the frost forming on the loose curly hair around his cheek.

"Thanks," I said.

Then his teeth flashed a bright smile in the moonlight and then he started giggling.

"What?" I said hesitantly. I wasn't quite sure what he found so funny.

He started laughing outright saying, "Oh, that was priceless! The way you got off the train! Oh, girl! You had everyone so shocked, they nearly froze in their ski-doo boots!"

My smile slowly disappeared as I said, "What do you mean? Are you making fun of me? What did I say that was so funny?"

Now, he was shrugging and waving his arms, "Oh, no, no, no... it wasn't so much what you said, it was how you said it, almost absent-minded, proper-prissy type... well, you know... the 'thank you.' No wonder you drove Fred crazy!"

Well, I didn't know... I did what? I was rather offended. I turned around and continued walking. I drove Fred crazy? What on earth did he mean by that!

I heard him coming up behind me almost on a run before I realized that I had been walking too fast. I slowed down. We were nearing the cabin when I stopped and turned around again.

He put the suitcase down and I said, "I'm sorry, Ron. I'm just not myself. What did you mean crazy? Has Fred gone crazy?"

Then he said, "Janine, don't you ever say you're sorry to me. I don't ever want you to be sorry about something to me, understand? Let us keep it the same now as it has always been between us; just open honesty, trust, and love. Don't ever be afraid to talk to me. Tell me how you feel. I'll understand, and you know that I'll always be here to help you if I can. I always have."

That was such a grand speech. I watched him wipe his long jet-black forehead curls back with both hands. He used to call them his "Elvis locks."

I smiled and whispered, "Thanks. Is Mother that sick and is Fred really crazy?"

He giggled again, "No, your mother isn't that sick. Just got a touch of pneumonia that's all. But, there was no one to look after her to get water, wood and such. And, Fred... well, hard to tell what's going on in his head. Won't talk to anyone anymore. I heard he was in a hospital in Toronto for an awful long time though. But, don't know what happened."

I was puzzled now, "But, where's O?"

Ron answered, "Well, his first wife died and now he has to take care of things. The boys went with him but they came back alone this morning. Your Mom couldn't go with O when he left. That was the day, she got sick."

I turned and started walking when he said, "Oh, by the way, did you get on at Armstrong?"

"No," I said, "Why?"

I heard him take a deep breath before he said, "Oh, my wife left last week and hasn't been back since. I thought maybe you would have seen her."

I kept walking and said, "No. I got on at Nakina... and no, I did not see her. Did you ever marry her?"

"Oh, no. No way she'd marry me!"

We stepped on to Mother's porch. As we neared the door, he whispered from behind me, "Janine, wait."

I stopped and turned only to feel his hand on my chin.

He said, "Be very careful. Old Henry says there's an evilness about. A strange spirit or something."

I froze and didn't get the chance to say anything as he pushed the door open in front of me. Just what on earth did he mean by that? I felt a smile touch my lips as I stepped in. Silly guy! The heat nearly knocked me back. Oh, my, was it ever hot in the room! The stove was red hot and mother was in a fever with a very bad cold at the corner of the room on the double bed. I didn't even notice Ron leave, for it was a good ten minutes before I got Mother a bit more comfortable. I kept thinking that it was really strange that Ron would say that. What evilness? Why would he say that? I've never known Ron to be superstitious.

In between her coughing fits, Mother informed me that the rotten scoundrel took off on her and only sent the kids back for her to look after. Well, where were they? I no sooner had that thought when the door burst open. They were all over me, yapping about something at the same time. Finally, things got a bit more down to normal and I began to take notice of them. Benny, the taller one was definitely now almost as tall as I was but Lenny was more stockier than tall. Funny about these twins, if you could not tell them apart before, their bodies certainly left no doubt now. I no longer had to guess whom I was addressing when I asked Benny why his father decided not to come home. We were outside splitting and bringing in wood for the stove. He was certain his father had not gone back to the town where the house was. He had to go somewhere else, something to do with a will, and something in a bank somewhere. That was why that explanation meant nothing to Mother. She wouldn't have a clue what that was about.

As I was chiselling the ice, widening the hole around the water hole, Lenny came down with the water-pail and I asked him if he had heard where his father was off to when he did not come back. He said O told him that he was going to Savant Lake about a will or something and then to a bank in Fort William somewhere and that he'd be back as soon as he fixed things up. I decided that I'd to go to the store and call Savant Lake in the morning.

The black and white dog met me as I was half way to the store the next day with Lenny and Benny behind me. It was so good to see him. His tail wagged as he licked the "skin off my gloves" as the boys said. I petted his head and told him how wonderful it was to be back, and how glad I was to see him. The boys laughed and snickered behind me.

I called the store owner in Savant Lake where O did his shopping and kept a mail box. The telephone rang. The Groundhogs were standing there anticipating my words as I pretended to be a secretary of some kind.

At the fourth ring, a man answered and I said, "Good afternoon, Sir. I am inquiring as to the whereabouts of a certain Mr. Hugh Sigmondson. Has he been to see you recently?"

I flipped an imaginary scarf over my shoulder that got the boys clamping their hands over their mouths.

After a brief pause, the voice at the other end replied, "Yeah, he was here. I give the envelope to him like she said... his wife, I mean. Who's this?"

I ignored the question and said, "Thank you very much, Sir!"

I hung up the phone.

The Groundhogs broke into a sputter and soon they were rolling with imitations of my voice, "Thank you very much, Sir!"

I laughed with them as we doubled over in laughter behind the potato storage counter. The boys were still howling with laughter all the way home with their imitations of me. I thought that maybe O had some legal business to attend to, so I would have to stall Mother with all kinds of explanations. As we waited for him to return, I made Mother's favourite meals and I told her wonderful stories about the city.

As I soothed her forehead, brushing the hair away from her face, I noticed the black hair now lying a solid dark grey across her forehead and temples. Her dark brown eyes looked into mine. With a jolt of shock, I suddenly felt like I was looking down into my own pair of eyes! To cover up my reaction, I immediately bent forward and kissed her on the forehead and gave her a hug. Her arms closed around me and for the very first time in my entire life, I actually felt her hugging me! I gave her a quick kiss on her cheek and then I was out the door with the two boys behind me.

As I stood by the water hole and listened to the noise of the community, I began thinking that nothing was fair in this world. You never get what you feel you deserve. There wasn't a thing you could do to prevent bad things from happening to you. You paid a horrific price for some ghastly outcomes and lost some immensely precious things without having had anything to do with them or have any say whatsoever! My mother was sent away to a sanatorium for tuberculosis treatment when I was about six. She was gone for about five years, and came back with one lung less to a child who didn't know her. I was raised by my two older sisters. I never knew a mother's love when I was a child. But, my mother was still here. I still had time. One hug at a time. I have been doing a lot of thinking lately. Thinking back at myself. Taking a good look at myself and trying to understand me.

O finally came home in such great spirits that none of the tongue lashing he got from Mother seemed to dim his happiness. He sat the boys down beside Mother and told them the story about the stocks and bonds he had accumulated over the years and had given to his wife. And low and behold, she had willed them all back to him for the boys.

The boys all yelled, "We are rich! We are rich!"

I smiled.

From then on O was treated like royalty and he settled down on the bed beside Mother. The boys ran around doing his bidding.

The next day, just before I went out the door to return to Thunder Bay, I bent close to O's ear as he was handed another cup of tea in bed, and whispered for only him to hear, "If I see you still in bed being waited on hand and foot when I come back in the spring, I will personally launch you out onto a chunk of ice straight out to the middle of the lake, do you hear me?"

For the first time in all the years since he had been here with Mother, he grabbed my hand and pulled me forward and I heard him say, "If I had ever had a daughter of me own, Janine, I could not have wished for a better daughter than you!"

Generous mood, eh! Making a face at him, I shrugged and pulled away. But, then I met his eyes for a full minute before I stood up. I had always thought that he didn't like me, that he was always hell-bent to get rid of me, and then he says that? I smiled to myself, and without comment, I turned and walked out. The Groundhogs were behind me, each taking turns with my suitcase. Yeah, there he was to meet us and walk us to the train station, the old dog.

You are lucky. I felt sorry for you. I was going to take your mother too, you know? But, now is not the time. A time will come when you will want me, my lost little one. You will want only me... only me... only me...

128

CHAPTER *17*

When I got off the train at Sioux Lookout, I headed straight to the hotel. The woman at the desk didn't even glance at me as I paid for the room and walked up the stairs. As I stepped in to the hallway, my heart suddenly flipped, for the door in front of me opened and out came Fred! His eyes widened as he saw me. I could feel my body moving and then I was on the floor kneeling and he was pushing my head down, getting the blood to rush back into my head. With one arm through my elbow, he led me to the number on the key that he took from me. I sat down on the bed, and without a word, he started pulling off my boots and taking off my coat, and I just lay down on the bed. Then he was there with a wet cloth and I froze as he sat down beside me and began wiping the warm cloth across my face. I had clamped my jaw shut so hard it began to ache. I remained like that with just my eyes following him around the room. Then he was pulling the woolen blanket over me from the foot of the bed.

Suddenly, I came to life, throwing back the blanket, I jumped up, yelling, "What the hell are you doing? Just what do you think you're doing! Get out! Get out!"

He took one look at me and turned to the door and went out. The door clicked behind him and I heard his footsteps going down the stairs. I lay back down and waited. I swore I could see my heart beating against the blanket tucked so close around my chest. My thoughts alternated between panic and excitement, and then nothing but plain white searing anger! Still, I waited. I waited until I got so drowsy that I found myself trying to blink away the weight from my eyelids. A stupid thought settled into my brain that the sand-man had planted his solid butt on top my eyelids! I never for the life of me, ever imagined seeing Freddy again! Fred, oh, heavens! I knew I still loved him the split second that I saw him! I could feel the tears rolling down my face as I realized the situation I was in.

* * * *

Fred sat in the restaurant. He didn't just leave her out there, you know. He had been chasing a man whom he thought was the man who was sneaking around their cabin. You see, someone had been at the trapper's shack. The man used to come once in a while and he could never catch him. He was sure Charlie knew someone was around too. Anyway, he was trying to find out about a puppy when he heard a guy saying that the worst part for mosquitoes was the swamp by Clay River. Then he started thinking about how would that guy know about that place? Nobody goes there without first passing his place. He went to see the guy and low and behold, it was that strange guy who popped up once in awhile at the village—that Nisha or whatever they call him! The guy up and left. So, he went after him, and then he got beat up bad. All of a sudden a bunch of men just popped up around him and beat the heck out of him. He was sick a long time. Lots of broken ribs, punctured lung and other stuff. Eventually he got out of the hospital in Toronto. Charlie was in Thunder Bay by then, so he went there. That's where he saw that guy again. He thought it was the guy but the man took off before he could catch him or see his face, for sure. Then he flew out to the trap-line again to take the stuff that he had bought. Couldn't leave them sitting in the shack at the village too long. When he finished putting his traps away, he went back to Thunder Bay and then he saw the same guy again, so he followed him. He knew the man would find Charlie. Sure enough, there she was. The man didn't hang around because he'd seen him. The next day, he went there again across the street from Charlie's place and waited for the man and see what he does when he sees Charlie coming home. He stayed a couple of times, watching the man watching Charlie. The man never did a thing. Just watched her come home. He didn't think the man would hurt her but he was sure he was the one causing him all this grief and pain. Meaning that he sure had been having some close calls. The guy was smart, real smart. Nobody comes near his place without him knowing, but this guy, maybe he even helped himself to a cup of tea when he was right there! In the winter time, the spook goes away. Doesn't like to leave any tracks. But, then that's not counting the weird attraction he'd been having on wolves, bears, ravens and such. Fred sighed, maybe he ought to go talk to her and tell her his side of things. Would she listen? Maybe not. Maybe, he was just plain going crazy.

Talk about crazy; it's Old Henry. He was at the store in the community recently when Old Henry came in. His glassy eyes settled on Fred as he sat down on the bench beside the door. Damn crazy old Indian! He really gave him the spooks! Does it on purpose too, the old coot!

After he got a few groceries and was heading out the door, the old coot sticks out his cane to block his way and he says, "See that old dog that always hangs around you? That's him! That's him, I tell you!"

Fred could see the old black and white dog outside through the window, just standing there. Man, he don't know now who was crazier, him or Old Henry!

* * * *

I heard footsteps coming up the stairs and then there was a knock at the door. I jumped up and opened it and there stood Fred.

"You know we have to talk. If you don't want to talk to me, then please hear me out because I need to tell you a few things."

I backed away from the door, determined not to open my mouth again. I sat down by the table and indicated the other chair for him.

He sat there fidgeting for the longest time before he finally blurted out, "I don't know if you will believe me or not, but it doesn't matter now. I never told you things because I thought you wouldn't believe me anyway. Maybe I should have just told you. Anyway, I have made mistakes one after the other. I guess I don't need to tell you that, but I have nothing left now but to tell you the truth."

I kept my eyes down on my clasped hands on my lap. He cleared his throat several more times before he took a deep breath and rushed out a bizarre tale, that... no, I probably would not have believed if he had told me then.

Fred had apparently been hunting for "our invisible man" and had gotten very close when he was suddenly beaten totally out of commission for a quite long time. That was about the time when I had my crazy snow machine ride in the middle of the night. This meant that no one would ever know who the person was until Fred himself caught him. I shuddered. So, there was someone out there at the trap-line. Why hadn't Fred ever said anything? When did he find out that there was someone out there with us? Questions were starting to race around in my head again. It was at those times when I became totally oblivious to anyone and everyone around me. I was remembering one night at the trap-line late in October when winter finally set in.

Fred and I were laying in bed watching the flickering lights against the ceiling from the fire in the wood-stove, when he had asked, "Did your parents ever talk about the legends of long ago?"

I had repeated, "legends?"

I could feel him turn to look at me, "Yes."

I smiled in the dark saying, "Well, I don't know, but when we were kids we used to hear all about Weesquachak's exploits and all the tricks he would pull on the birds and animals and doing things to the people. He was really funny at times."

There was silence for quite a while after my voice faded. Then he had asked, "What would you think if we had Weesquachak pestering us here in the summer?"

I remember I laughed and said, "There are no young ladies here to lure or some hapless little animal to trick!"

I thought he had just been teasing me. Had he actually thought back then that there was someone sneaking around our cabin? What about the shirt? The canoe? The wood-pile? The curly black strands of hair. No! That was ridiculous!

Suddenly, I became aware of Fred's voice in conversational tone saying, "...and the dog danced in shoes with shiny silver twinkle toes, and the moon laughed as a lady bug glued itself to the dog's nose."

He stopped as he turned from the window and saw that I was watching him.

I said in a serious tone, "Don't you go crazy on me, please."

He laughed and said, "I just wanted to know if you were even listening to me. You didn't answer me. I asked if you felt like you are still my wife?"

I could feel anger creeping up my throat again and I swallowed hard and said, "That is not what we are here to talk about. I want you to tell me why you piled the wood on the top of my clothes-line pole, knowing that when I pulled it, it would all come crashing down on me. I want to know why you accused me of so many things, like the shirt that I lost, and whose hair was that caught on the branch. It was not yours and it was not mine! I want to know..."

His voice cut in, "Who planted that huge connibear trap right where I would step? Who put the big hole in the canoe? Who...."

His voice died.

I looked at him in disbelief as all that registered in my brain. What? He was looking at me like he was witnessing the most fascinating and totally horrifying thing on earth.

He shook his head, saying in a whisper, "You didn't?"

I heard my voice saying, "No. It wasn't you?"

We both shook our heads. This was absolutely crazy. Maybe, I had gone just as crazy as him and didn't know it! This was too much to take. I couldn't deal with this information right now. Suddenly, he stood up and glanced around like the walls were closing in on him.

He walked to the door and paused, saying, "You did not answer my question."

What was his question? Do I still feel like his wife?

I looked at him and then down at my hands, and I said in a voice that came just above a whisper, "Yes, I will always be your wife, Fred."

With that, he went out and closed the door behind him. I spent the rest of the night going over every single painful episode of our time together in the bush. But, I just could not, would not, accept the explanation that a Weesquachak figure was responsible for it all! That was like someone telling me that I was, after all, one of the three little pigs! Wait, what was Ron's warning about? What did he say... "there is an evilness afoot," or something like that. If there was an evil presence about, I still firmly believed that if it could leave a foot print, it could also be caught! The next morning, after a fretful night, I left the hotel and boarded the train back to the city without another word from Fred.

A week later, right after work, I had no sooner arrived home to my old apartment in Thunder Bay when I noticed that the man was out there again! He wore the same long dark-brown overcoat that Freddy used to have. He called it his "city coat." He said he had lost it and I knew now that it could not have possibly been Fred all those times out there. Now, a new fear came over me. I had not been that scared thinking that it was Fred out there but now, I knew that there was a strange man out there watching me! I did not know what to think. I went about my daily business and tried not to think about things and consequences.

Had I misjudged Fred all that time? Why had he not said anything? Why did he not tell me about the footprints at the time? Why had I not told him about the things that I saw? Why had I not asked him about the things that he was accusing me of? I wish we had learned to talk to each other. I wished that I had learned to show love and affection more. I wished that I could have found it in me to tell him how much I loved him, and most of all, it was knowing that, had I been able to do all those things, my baby would be alive.

The man still stood out on the street watching my window. I could never get a clear view of him and it soon drove me to distraction. I would sit in my living-room knowing he was out there. I would make my supper knowing he was out there. I was getting very paranoid and jumpy.

Then, my work contract ran out. So, I paid another month's rent and decided to go home and see how Mother was doing before I looked for another job.

Hah! He thinks he knows me, then? But, my sweet lovely one, I will hand you your lost one on a cedar bed platter, but only when I feel you are ready. Just wait...

CHAPTER *18*

That night in Sioux Lookout, I kept having nightmares about the dark shadow of the man materializing in front of me every time I turned! It was nearly close to train time when I awoke the next morning and discovered that I was not well. I must have caught the flu or something as I definitely had a fever. I got to the train station on time and sat in the waiting room gasping in quick short breaths until the train came. There was pain in my chest. It did occur to me that since I was there, perhaps I should have gone to the hospital, but all I wanted to do was to curl up somewhere and sleep forever and never wake up.

I slept most of the way home. I was feeling very light-headed as I stepped off the train and walked on rather shaky legs to the store and into the post office.

The postal clerk had just dumped the morning mail on to the counter and said, "Janine, are you alright?"

"I have the flu or something. I feel terrible right now, but I'll probably be fine after a nap. Is Mother home?"

He paused a moment and said, "Oh, you're losing your voice. You sound bad. No, your mother's not home. They left for the bush. She said they wouldn't be back until after break-up. But, she left a key in your mailbox. In case someone came back she said."

I took the house key from the envelope and I thanked the man and slowly made my way through the store. Two of the older men from the community were leaning on the counter, smoking and talking about spring hunting spots. I smiled and nodded at their glances of welcome and pushed the door open.

I stepped out of the store and realized that there was no way I was going to be able to carry my suitcases all the way to the other end of the community to Mom's place. My chest was aching, my throat hurt and I had one huge splitting headache! There were six kids fooling around and wrestling on the hill at the corner of the store. To the side of the path, was a small sleigh with a wooden box nailed on top. My suitcases would fit into the box perfectly.

I yelled to the kids, "Hey, who's sleigh is this?"

Johnny came running. He was Ron's nephew and quite a big boy now. He'd be about ten or twelve years old.

I said, "I'm not feeling very well, do you think you can pull my suitcases on your sleigh? I'll pay you."

His face broke into a big grin, "Oh, yeah, sure!"

He ran and got the sleigh and heaved my suitcases onto it and I followed him down the path along the railroad tracks. I listened to him prattle on about this and that, telling me about everything that had happened to every single person in the community since I had left. I began thinking, why did I have to pick one that talked and talked so much! He suddenly quieted down as he began to pant with his effort to get up the hill over the path by the railroad tracks. Then he ran as the little sleigh bounced along behind him, down the hill to the creek. I followed in long strides behind him, trying to keep up as I gasped for breath.

It was as I was finally catching up with him when he slowed to get up the hill that I heard him saying, "And he was going to kill somebody!"

I paused a moment before I asked, "Who was going to kill someone?"

He waited for me on the top of the hill before he answered, "Your Freddy!"

Oh, I was feeling awful. I wasn't even going to ask whom he'd want to kill. At that point, I really didn't care. We were nearing the cabin when my brain spat out the word that had stuck. My Freddy? There it was again. Why was he always "my Freddy." I looked to the side at the long wide bay where the village lay. Yes, from now until forever, according to "them" I would always be Freddy's and he was my Freddy! Until one of us married someone else.

I unlocked the door and Johnny brought the suitcases in. Our breath hung in the cold air of the room. I walked to Mother's bed in the corner and threw myself down thinking that I would start the fire later. I reached into my pocket for some money when I heard Johnny at the stove. I watched him quickly locate Mother's fire-starter box where she kept paper, birch-bark, wood shavings and splints. Next went in the smaller pieces of chopped up wood. O always left the wood ready for lighting. I watched Johnny and soon he had a good fire going. He came and stood beside me. I reached into my pocket and gave him a bill.

"I can get you some water too!" he said.

I looked up at his rosy cheeks and said, "If Mom left last week, that water hole would be frozen over solid. I doubt they'd leave the chisel out there and I'd have to look around for the old axe."

"Oh, I'll get water!"

He turned and went out the door with the water-pail. I could hear the pail rattling inside the wooden box on his sleigh. The room was beginning to warm up so I made one more effort to make myself a bit more comfortable. I hauled up one suitcase to the bed and took out two chocolate bars that I had in there and left them on the table for Johnny along with another two dollars change I had in my pocket. I think I gave him a dollar already. I pulled a comforter from the corner and threw it over me. I must have dozed off.

It was some time later when I heard Johnny coming back in. I looked at my watch. He must have been gone for about an hour.

I had to swallow several times before I managed to say, "Where did you go, to Armstrong for the water?"

He was struggling with the water-pail, trying not to bump the bottom as he put it on the shelf against the wall beside the door.

He giggled as he came towards me beaming, "No! I had to take the path around the point and into the little bay to my grandmother's water hole. Ron isn't home either, you know. So, Grandma and Grandpa are you're closest neighbours. Everybody's gone spring hunting."

He had gone all that way for the water, no wonder he was gone so long!

I pointed to the chocolate bars and the change on the table and said, "Take those. How much did I give you the first time?"

He grabbed the chocolate bars and stuffed the change into his pocket and mumbled through the dark chocolate that was now gushing out between his teeth as he smiled, "Five. You gave me five the first time, now I've got seven. Thanks, Janine! I'll bring in some more wood too before I go, okay?"

I smiled. The little rascal! I had been feeling bad thinking that I had only given him three dollars for his efforts. I let him bring in several more loads of wood before he got set to go home. I asked him to bring me a glass of water and he threw several more logs into the fire before the door closed behind him. Then I was alone.

I woke up late in the evening and the room had cooled down quite a bit. My head spun as I sat up. I have to keep the fire going or I'll never be able to start it again. I kept the quilt around me as I slowly made my way across the floor to the stove. There were still some glowing embers at the vent and I threw in some paper and twigs before I put the split wood in, with several round pieces on top. The fire started again almost immediately and I crawled back into bed.

It was totally dark when I next awoke. I found the matches on the table but I was shaking so badly, I nearly dropped the glass lamp chimney as I lit the coal-oil lamp. The water cup was empty and there was only a small glow of embers through the stove vent. I sat on the bench by the table for quite awhile before I could muster enough energy to cross the floor. I put the last log into the stove and fell against it. I became frightened. What if the stove had been hot, I could have burnt myself! I turned to the water-pail. I had to get back into bed. With concentrated effort, I carried the cup of water back to the bed and I laid down like I weighed a ton.

Fire! The house was burning down! I'm burning! I threw off my blankets and the cold air jolted me awake. I had been dreaming! I was very hot. I knew I had a high fever. I could see the stove clearly and it was almost dawn. I decided I'd look for some aspirins later and rolled over, hugging the pillow to me.

I fought my way through another thick nightmare and opened my eyes. The light was coming from the front window. It must have been midday. I knew I should get up and make the fire. But, I only took a sip of water and lay back down. I could see my breath in the air. It was very cold in here. When I next awoke, I was suffocating from the heat inside the quilt. I was having trouble breathing and somewhere within me was fear. I should get up and get the fire going. I need some aspirins or something. I don't have any more water left in the cup... but I couldn't get my body to obey my order to get out of bed.

Out of the darkness of my dreams, I heard a snow machine come to a stop outside the door. The door opened and a light went across my closed eyes. I rolled into a ball to escape the noise, the searing light and the oppressive heat.

In the clutches of unforgiving nightmares, I struggled with thick hot animals at my throat and chest, and the smell of cedar was almost overwhelming as the animals continually dragged me into their dark hot caves. Then, there was a smell like someone was burning grass fires around me, and the sound of a soothing chanting voice, and then at times, there was cold, blessed cold water was on my face. I was so thirsty, I wished I could just catch some of that rain into my mouth.

I felt someone's hair under my hand. The hair flowed softly between my fingers. My eyes opened and my hand became still. I stared at the wooden roof beams above me as I slowly removed my hand from the head. I looked down. It was Fred. He was asleep, leaning against the bed with his head down beside me on the mattress. Oh, my love! I was overcome and wracked with uncontrollable sobbing. I cried as I hugged my knees to my chest. Strong arms held me tightly as my body threatened to break into pieces before the blackness came again.

When I next awoke, it was daylight and I smelled chicken noodle soup. I was hungry. I opened my eyes. Fred was in front of the stove. He had his back to me and I watched his slumped shoulders roll as he stirred a pot. His hair was neatly combed. He looked all muscle, and not at all skinny as he was the last time I saw him. I closed my eyes when he turned. I heard him come to the table. Then he was beside me again. He lifted the quilt and my eyes flew open as sharp cold air hit my skin. He removed a hot pad off my chest that I didn't even know was there. I did not move and he was so intent in what he was doing that I watched his face as he replaced the hot cedar poultice on my chest. His hand was coming up to my forehead when his eyes locked to mine. His hand paused before he touched my forehead and brushed my hair back.

I made several attempts before I could get my voice to work, and I said, "I was dreaming that hot animals kept pasting themselves to my chest and I couldn't pull them off and then there was smoke, a grass fire that was going to burn me alive."

He leaned over and kissed me on the forehead and whispered, "You're fever's gone. Are you hungry?"

I nodded. My head felt very light but I pulled myself up in bed as he shoved pillows behind me. I looked down to see that I was wearing Mother's nightgown. How?

He saw my gaze and he said, "You were sweating buckets and I had to change the gowns on you several times."

I looked at him as he dished out the soup at the table and he continued, "I thought that the other night, I might take you to the hospital, but then I figured it would do more damage dragging you around outside and into the train for a five hour trip to the hospital. So, I was right that I didn't take you anywhere, eh? Now, you're going to be fine."

He smiled as he put a bowl on my lap.

I asked, puzzled, "The other night? How long have you been here?"

"Let's see. I left the trap-line Monday, stopped to repair the old machine at Whitewater Lake. I got in on Tuesday night. I stopped at the store and they told me that you had come in on the Monday morning train. Then Johnny was hanging around my machine when I came out and he told me that you were sick. So, I came over after I dumped the pelts and traps at the cabin. Eat your soup before it gets cold."

I slowly sipped the first tablespoon before I asked, "What day is it?"

He smiled before saying, "Thursday morning."

My spoon stopped mid-way to my mouth as I blinked in shocked silence. Two days! I had lost two days? I looked at his flashing brown eyes. He looked tired.

"You mean I spent two days fighting those hot furry animals off my chest?"

He smiled, nodding as he ate his soup, "They made you well."

I said, "And the smoke, what was the grass fire that was threatening to burn me?"

He smiled, "That was cedar branches on the stove."

Suddenly, feeling uncomfortable, I put my head down and began, "I'm sorry I put you to so much trouble, you didn't have to."

Suddenly, he was kneeling beside me saying, "Don't. Don't let us start that again, okay? Leave things be. Everything is fine. You are well. I am here. I will be here until you tell me to go... alright?"

I nodded.

I had another bowl of soup as he brought in more wood. He told me stories as he went about the inside chores. I watched, listened, and periodically dozed off during the day. By evening, I insisted on going outside to the outhouse. He walked with me and stood outside. Strangely, I felt no embarrassment at the sudden turn of events. He seemed totally at ease. I too felt strangely comfortable now. We had reached somewhere. I did not understand this at all. But, it was okay.

By Sunday, I felt quite strong although he continued to stay with me in the cabin. He slept on my old single bed by the window while I remained on Mother's double bed in the main room. We played cards in the afternoons and some evenings he went to his cabin to pack for the spring. He informed me that he had only come to town to do his spring shopping and sell some furs.

On Monday night after we had gone to bed, we talked to each other across the dark room.

I said, "The days are getting very warm. You have to leave soon. Don't worry about me, I'll be alright. I have been thinking of going to Winnipeg."

There was no response in the darkness and soon I fell asleep.

He got on the train early Tuesday morning for his supplies. I was quite surprised when he came back on the evening train. He came in with a big smile on his face.

I said, "What are you doing here? I didn't expect you back until..."

That did not come out the way I wanted it to.

He came and sat down beside me at the table saying, "I only went to Savant Lake. That's where I do my business now. I don't know anybody there, no old drinking buddies to bother me. I quit drinking."

I looked at him. Maybe that was the change I've noticed in him. Or, was it a change that had to do with me getting sick. He was comforted in knowing that he had been there when I needed someone... this time. I watched him, thinking that it was going to be very painful when I leave him. This time, it would be me who was leaving. Did I really want to go?

Then, Fred asked softly, "Why are you looking at me like that?"

I shook my head and said, "I know you too well now. You are up to something, what is it?"

He threw his head back and laughed out loud. I felt my heart skip. It had been such a long time since I had heard Fred laugh like that. He was the Fred I used to know as a kid. He was the Fred I loved.

I continued to look at him as he turned and faced me, "I bought something for you."

I took a slow deep breath and said, "Fred, I don't want anything from you. I don't need anything."

He shook my shoulders as he said, "No, listen. I bought you a gun. Your own .22."

I looked at him stupidly before I whispered, "A gun? What for?"

Again, the grin spread over his face, "So, we can go hunting! Come with me to the trap-line. We'll go hunting and fishing. I'll show you how to shoot down the ducks in mid-flight! I'll teach you a thing or two about fishing. And you can have all the peace and quiet that you need right now."

"Wait!" I interrupted, "What do you know about what I need and I probably know more about catching fish than you do and as for shooting ducks, I'm probably a better shot than you are! You just never gave me the chance."

His face was about a foot from mine as he said, "Yeah?"

I answered, "Yeah. You never knew that because you never gave me the chance and besides I was too busy playing housewife. But, I could never do that again, Fred. I couldn't do it ever again."

He smiled and stuck out his hand. "It's a deal. Come with me to the trap-line, only as a friend, only as a hunting and fishing buddy. That's all."

Was that possible? I smiled, shaking my head. I didn't know. But, what else was there for me to do? I had nowhere to go. Right now, I just wanted to disappear somewhere for a while and I guess the trap-line was the best place for that.

I looked at him and said, "If you can keep your distance, I can keep mine."

He smiled and said, "It's a deal."

I knew that this arrangement would become a battle of stubborn wills but that would be my strongest assurance. Neither of us would admit to being weaker; neither of us would give in. That was the best guarantee possible.

I smiled and asked, "When?"

"Right now! Just bring your bag, leave your suitcases here and we'll go to my cabin. I still have your ski-doo suit and your bush clothes there."

I looked around the cabin feeling quite dazed by the turn of events but this time determined that I was going to live. I looked straight at him. I felt no tension or apprehension, just an old friend standing there in front of me, giving me a chance to breathe, giving me a place to recover. Huh! Life was strange.

He returned my gaze and then I nodded. I could do this.

Ah, now, wait! This is not supposed to happen! Oh, these humans are unpredictable creatures! Fred is no problem, he's easy to manipulate, but the girl... can't reach that girl. She is too far away. Her... her spirit... no, her intuition... no, her knowledge... no, her acknowledgement—is lacking. That's it! She is too far away from her culture, I can't reach her! If she does not know I'm here, how can I reach her! Hmm, I must use that stupid man as a bridge... I can trick her into... yes, yes, that's the plan. I am just so smart and cunning. I am so smart, so smart, so smart... Hey, wait! I notice I am having some kind of difficulty here. Why are my words going into replay as I'm changing form? It's like my brain is bumping along with my burping body... body... body...

CHAPTER *19*

I rode behind him on the snow machine with the loaded sleigh behind us. Down the path, across the railroad tracks and down into the portage road. Strangely, this road was well used by people getting wood, people out setting traps, snares, or just out ice-fishing on the lakes along the road. I cried when I came to the spot where I had lost the baby's water. I tightened my grip around Fred's middle. I wondered if he ever thought of the things that were going through my mind.

We stopped for a meal on an island at Smoothrock Lake. It was quite dark and we built a fire and warmed up a bit and made a pot of tea. After a quick midnight lunch of bologna sandwiches and hot tea we were back on the snow machine again. I was unusually quiet but he made no comment. Perhaps he knew what I was going through in retracing my steps through this route. When we entered Whitewater Lake, I remembered the excitement of my first trip into this lake. I was so naive and hopeful of a bright and happy future, so full of love and life. I wondered now how I would be when next I came back this way.

It was dawn when we entered Clay Lake. We were just coming to the point where the cabin was, when the sun came up over the horizon. Fred slowed to a stop and shut off the engine and we sat perfectly still watching the big orange sun. For some reason, I had such a strong urge to cry. I covered my sudden emotional reaction by swinging my leg off the seat and stomped around behind the sleigh, trying to get some circulation back into my feet. I turned to see Fred spread-eagled in the snow beside the machine. He was making a snow angel! He smiled and I said nothing as I flopped down in the snow beside him at a good two arm's length away from him. I swung my arms and legs into a wide arch and started giggling.

How ridiculous we must look!

We were back on the machine and headed to the cabin when we came across a trail in the snow. It was a wolf.

I found the cabin the same as I had left it. It seemed like I had been gone a very long time, but there it stood, looking just the same. Fred pushed the door open and I entered behind him. I saw a single bed in the corner of the room beside the stove. There was bedding on the bed and a small shelf had been nailed to one of the logs above it. Someone had been here with him. He saw me looking at the bed while he was getting the fire going and then he stopped and threw his head back and gave a deep belly laugh.

Indicating the bed, he said, "A high school drop-out. One of the boys who decided to quit school and become a trapper like his dad was. Well, the mother asked me to take him here with me and teach him the ropes. The very first day... no, the very first half-hour after we got here, I asked him to split some more wood while I got the water hole opened up again. I was coming up the path with the water-pail, when I saw him just as he was swinging his axe down on a block of wood propped up like a see-saw. Well, it was too late. Before I could shout, he hit the block of wood too far out to the edge and the wood spun upward and hit him square on the forehead and knocked him out cold! He just fell back like a log. The tea wasn't even hot on the stove when I decided to turn around, right then and there and take him back home. I was just scared what he was going to do to himself next. Oh, you should have seen the huge hockey puck that was popping out from between his eyes. Anyway, the kid would not hear of it because of what he could see growing on his forehead when he crossed his eyes. By morning he had two huge black eyes and still swelling besides the huge lump he was sporting on his forehead!"

I found that I was laughing along with him as he gestured, imitating the poor kid.

When I had stopped to pull off my snow-boots, he continued, "He tried to help out here and there, but he was so clumsy. I gave him some rabbits to skin and maybe a few muskrats but, he just wasn't interested. He basically just waited until the bruises were gone before he allowed me to take him back home. When I went back to the community later on, I found out he had gone back to school after all."

I glanced at him and smiled, "So, one day when he becomes a doctor or a lawyer... or a veterinarian, he has you to thank?"

Fred laughed and said, "I doubt it. I don't think he liked me very much after that month and a half that he stayed here."

That was the longest conversation that I had ever had with Fred inside these four walls. I grabbed the chisel and went out to get some water. From now on, I will do as I please. I don't owe him anything, I will not do as I believe he would want me to do. I will do as I want to do!

As I stood there gradually widening the water hole, I saw in the distance a small dot making its way across the lake. It was the wolf. By the time, I got back with the water, Fred had the fire roaring full blast. He made the tea while I went to bring in more wood.

Next came the on-going setting and checking of traps and then the preparations for the spring hunt. I didn't think it important but Fred insisted that I keep track of what I caught so I could get my share of the money when he went to sell them.

I came in from bringing a couple loads of logs with the snow machine and I threw my jacket on the bed. The stew pot was slowly bubbling on the stove. Fred sure made delicious stew. I still had a few pelts to stretch so I got up on the stump that we used for a chair and peered over the wooden shelves strung along the ceiling. As I was pushing aside muskrat boards to get at some smaller beaver stretching racks, I saw a roll of moose-hide. Fred came in with some frozen fish which he threw into the sink beside the stove.

I pulled the moose-hide off the nail and asked, "When did you kill this one?"

He looked up from the table where he had begun stretching some mink skins, and said, "Oh, in the fall. I cut off the hair, scraped off the flesh, and scraped it on the stretcher just before Christmas... and that was all I did with it. I brought it in and kind of just let it dry like that."

We had long since stopped talking in English altogether. Now, our conversations were mostly in Ojibway.

I looked at the roll of moose-hide and said, "Tell you what. Let's work on this together and when it's done, I'll make us some new mitts, mukluks, and moccasins. Providing you help me with all the pulling when it comes to the softening process."

He laughed and said, "I remember my father and mother doing that. They used to sit foot to foot on the floor and they would rotate pulling the hide around and around and each time my mother pulled, we would watch to see how far Father's butt would rise off the floor!"

I laughed. It was so nice to talk and laugh with him.

Then I said, "Remember the story of Weesquachak when he was a woman and became the third wife of a hunter? The two women were pulling the hide like that and Weesquachak lost his grip and he fell backwards, his spread legs flying up in the air and the women across from him saw his male genitals."

My smile disappeared and Fred's straight face looked back at me. We both remembered.

A month later, we had the leather all made and we even smoked it into an even beige shade. Then, some of the fur we trapped went into the cuffs of the mitts, moccasins and mukluks. I loved the layers of muskrat skins on my feet. They were a lot better than socks. I made all his things first and by the time I had finished my pair of mitts, I was running out of beads. I had only what I had left after that cradle we had made for the baby. It still hung in the corner by the double bed. I remembered when he was bending the bottom curve of the wood, it had slipped from his hand and slapped him on the cheek. Smack! I told him that it had a particularly soothing sound to it! I smiled at the memory.

I slept on that bed and Fred slept on the single bed beside the stove. He had asked if he should remove the cradle and put it elsewhere, but I shook my head. It looked like it belonged there. Someone just coming to visit might think that it was just a decoration, but I liked opening my eyes every morning and seeing it hanging there. It became a reminder of what would happen again if I dared to let myself get too physically close to Fred. It pained me that we immediately pulled away if one happened to come into contact with the other during the course of our everyday activities, but I knew that there could be no other way. I had said that if he could do it, then so could I. And, I was not going to be the one to give in first!

Spring came with the leaves coming out in one giant growing spree and the songs of the frogs filled the swamp and the shoreline around the cabin. The wolf that we had spotted when we first arrived, had kept a very curious eye on us. He never wandered far from our cabin. We kept an eye on the tracks. Once, I even went as far as to drag a half dozen suckers in a tub to the place he always come out of the bush and to the lake. I dumped the fish there and went back to the cabin before Fred came home. He only used the suckers for bait anyway.

If there was ever a time when I would have loved to have snuggled up in bed and listened to the frogs it was then. I found this the hardest; to be in one corner of the cabin and Fred in the other.

June came and we went swimming. That caused another problem not so much on my part but on his. I could not help having my shirt and pants sticking to my body when I stepped out of the water.

There were some funny times too. Like the time, he had just got out of the water and put his arms up over his head to dry his underarms, when I saw something flapping around under one arm. It was a huge bloodsucker! How I laughed at the sight of him trying to shake it off and trying to pull it off. I ended up prying it out with my fingernail. But, he could peel off his shirt at the hottest time of the day in the boat but I did not dare take off mine. After the first couple of times, we soon found that these were things we could do only when we were alone. We had to give each other a lot of space and time alone.

Then, the day came when we finally admitted that we just had to get back to the village. I needed supplies. We needed food. Fred needed things of his own. I had found that he went through a lot of tobacco but I never saw him smoke. Only that one time when we first went spring hunting, was when I had seen him with the pipe. I never saw it again. I did not know where he kept those things. It was none of my business. I too had my own bag of necessities that he did not poke around into.

It was sometime in the second week of June when we set out for the village in our canoe. We had asked Jason, the tourist guide to keep an eye on our place, and then we left.

We took our time crossing Whitewater Lake and camped out overnight at the point on Best Island. The mosquitoes were just horrible! After choking on blackflies as we tried to get the fire going, we dove into the tent and sprayed the last of the mosquito repellent to kill the giant blood-sucking mosquitoes that followed us in. I knew this place was bad at this time of year because of the swamp directly behind us, but oh, the beach was just gorgeous!

We left early the next morning and had lunch at the mouth of Loon Narrows. I told Fred stories about this place and in return, I heard stories about his family on the same location that I had known nothing about. I mentioned that when I was a child, I had remembered seeing a pair of dark shrivelled leather pieces that looked to have been a small pair of moccasins still tied together high up in a tree. He said that those had been the moccasins of his oldest brother who had died around this area at the age of five when Fred was only a baby, and the moccasins would have been hung up in a tree branch shoulder high. That would have been before I was born. We sat for a long time in silence. Our families had criss-crossed this region for many generations, yet we did not know each other's history.

We spent the rest of the time talking and reminiscing as we paddled the length of Smoothrock Lake. We pulled in late and slept at the big portage of Smoothrock Lake. The roaring river seemed so loud after the quiet solitude of the last several days and we had a visitor during the early hours. It was a bear cub and to my relief, there had been no sign of the mother around our camp-site.

We left early in the morning and paddled through the lakes and channels, rivers and portages, pretty much in silence until we came to the last rock cut.

Around the bend was the last portage and up the path about two and a half miles was the village. Fred stopped paddling and the canoe drifted for half the length of the bay. I waited. I did not move my paddle. I just waited. Then, I felt the dip and pull of his paddle away from the portage and into the channel. That would lead us to two more small portages along the railroad tracks that lead us into the lake at the village. He decided to come up to the community by canoe on the lake, rather than by portage with packsacks on our backs crossing the clearing in front of the store and down past the church to get to his cabin by the bay. Yes, I liked that better. I had not relished the idea of packsacks on my back, sweating and panting, across the railroad tracks, through the community, across the front of the store where people would come to the window and stare, down by the church, accompanied by children and barking dogs then down to the bay where we would finally reach Fred's cabin! This way was a lot more private, a lot more dignified, and a lot more peaceful.

When we arrived at the portage that crossed the railroad tracks, Fred pulled out the tent. No, he was not going to arrive late at night. We were going to camp here... one more night. We set up the tent and the smell from the tar of the railway ties was very strong. When the next train went by, the ground shook and the air was thick with train exhaust and tar smell. I took deep breaths and relished the smell of home! There seemed to descend upon us, a dampening effect. I watched and waited. Fred had become very quiet since we had set up the tent.

Finally, as we sat by the fire sipping the last of our coffee, he took a deep breath and said, "I'm sorry if I seem almost dead. I'm just so... scared. I'm afraid."

This was new. He was actually telling me what he was feeling!

I asked hesitantly, "Why?"

He took a deep breath.

Leaning against a tree and looking up into the sky he said, "Because, I'm afraid of what might happen, and that we may not come back down here together again."

I did not know what to say. I had been apprehensive too. I did not know if I was prepared to face Mother and pretend everything was alright.

I would be embarrassed if people found out that the only way we could get along was when we lived like brother and sister. I didn't think I could face them if they knew.

I kicked the heel of his boot that I could reach and said, "Hey. Nobody can hurt us unless we let them. If we stick close together and not let anybody come between us we'll be okay. We'll come back down this portage together again."

He turned and smiled at me. Then we had to dive into the tent to get away from the mosquitoes. This portage too, was in a swamp and just humming with huge mosquitoes at night!

CHAPTER 20

Early the next morning, we paddled out into the bay of the lake where our village was. Big white water-lilies bobbed in the waves of our canoe, sending out a fragrance that was better than the hundred dollar perfumes that I had smelled in the department stores. I put my head back, closed my eyes and took a long deep breath.

I heard Fred chuckling behind me, so I said, "Don't you ever think that there is a perfume better than this. You can't buy this!"

We paddled in silence to the community. As soon as we came around the channel, we could see the white cross of the Catholic Church in the clearing. Then we heard the dogs barking. The train went by like a long black and white garter snake all along the bay. It did not stop this morning. Then, silence descended with just the sea-gulls overhead, screeching at our paddles. Soon, we were past the island, past the dock, and into the bay beside his cabin.

We got off and pulled the canoe up. We unloaded the canoe and together we went up to see if the cabin was still in good shape. Fred whistled at how high the weeds were around the cabin and that he would have to cut them back. The cabin was still as we had left it though. As Fred swung the door open, the smell brought back memories. I set the outside campfire going.

I had the teapot steaming when Bob and his wife Sheila came down the path. Sheila said that they had seen the smoke from the campfire and being a Saturday, Bob was home, and she had in her arms a new baby! The bad memories of the last time I saw her disappeared as I looked down on the peaceful beautiful face of her baby!

Bob went inside the cabin where Fred was rummaging around

looking for a larger frying pan. Sheila sat down beside me. I poured the tea out for the men and handed Sheila a cup. Quite naturally, to free her hands, I took the baby into my arms. The weight of the baby in my arms and her natural tilt to my chest, brought out such an overwhelming emotion of intense pain that I found myself blinking back tears.

When Sheila had settled back kneeling on the ground, she asked in English, "Are you expectin' again?"

Quite taken aback and without warning, I answered, "Oh, no. We haven't got to there yet. We... we're still living like brother and sister."

I was feeling the warmth of the beautiful child in my arms when I realized what I had just said!

Then Sheila said, "I am just so glad our baby girl is still here. I was so afraid in the spring, she came down with such an awful cold, she couldn't breathe, and then her fever went up so high. Oh, I was in panic and tears, an' Bill was in Sioux Lookout, an' then Nisha shows up. Remember the guy I was tellin' you about last year? He says, Bill had told him he had tools for the motor. He just came by to fix that motor of Bill's that's always broken down. Well, I invites him in, while I go rummagin' in the shed he's got back there, and worryin' about the clothes if they are going to be dry in time for the train to the hospital. I mean my dress and the baby's diapers... I mean, I had been tendin' the baby day and night and never got time to do the washing... anyway, this Nisha, he just knocks on the door saying he needs the tools and then, he would watch her while I looked for them... and wouldn't you believe it! I came rushin' in, and there he was, standin' over the baby's crib. He had his hand on her head and I swear he was saying something... anyway he turns around... and, and, you know, I just can't explain it to this day. But, anyway, he just looks at me and says she'll be fine now. She doesn't need anything. She'll just sleep all night and she'll be right as rain, maybe even before the train comes in! Got the tools? I walks to the baby and him standin' there and I give him the tools and then, he goes out whistling a tune. An' you know? Her fever was gone and just like he said. She was gigglin' and kickin' up her feet by the time the train went by! Go figure! Eh, go figure! How do some people know them things! I am always so amazed that people can know them things!"

Just then Fred and Bob came out and sat down beside the fire. I did not say anything. What was she saying? Does she think that Nisha healed her baby? That sounded a bit too weird to me!

After plans were discussed about having supper together, Fred walked back to their cabin with them to get the axe that Bob had apparently borrowed last month. I found that English sounded so foreign now, after all this time of speaking in Ojibway! But, Bob and Sheila only spoke in English.

I had just cleared up the tea cups and pot from the campfire when Fred came back with the axe in his hand. I saw immediately that Fred had a furious look on his face. With a sense of total disappointment and betrayal, I took a deep breath and waited to hear what the problem was but he said not a thing. He walked right past me and down to the lake to get the rest of the things. I watched his back until he disappeared from view. I sighed, thinking that it's back to the old silent treatment again! The plan to keep communication open sure didn't last very long did it?

I yanked out a clean shirt and pants and got a clean towel from the box. I dug out from my bag a bar of soap and a bottle of shampoo that I had left in the cabin and headed out to the point of land by the high rock cliff. I knew that no one hung around there.

When I got to the rock point, the gentle waves were lapping at the rocks much the same as they did early this morning. The sun shone overhead and the sea-gulls circled around on their endless search for food. I kept my clothes on and dove into the deepest part of the bay. The water gurgled against my ears as I dove deeper into the water. I stayed down there to the count of thirty before I came up for air. I used to do that when I was a child. This summer I was able to count to over forty. I dove in several more times, before I just floated around staring at the sky.

I left the shampoo and soap on a rock close to the shore and helped myself to them until I felt it was close to supper-time. I had pulled myself up on the rock and stretched my arms to the sky, relishing the feel of the breeze against the wet clothes plastered to my body when I felt eyes watching me. I had been enjoying the luxury of washing with soap and shampoo that I was unaware that someone was watching. Now my eyes fell on Fred. He was sitting beside my clothes in the rock shade, watching me.

I went up the rock toward him. When I got near, he got up and walked past me and without a word, he stripped off his shirt, pants, and dove into the water. I smiled as I settled down on the rock to dry my hair. When I had combed out my hair, I watched him pull himself up onto a rock and stand up. I knew exactly how he felt as he turned his face to the sun and combed back his hair with his fingers. Something else touched me deep inside as I watched him coming up the sloping rock toward me. But, I distracted myself by running the brush through my hair once more. I had gotten so good at distracting myself.

He sat down beside me and I noticed that the goose-pimples from the cold water were still on his thighs as he sat back. He had never come this close to me before, dressed as he was now, with only his undershorts on! What was he doing?

I took a deep breath and asked, "So, what got you angry? After only half an hour here, you got angry at me about something. If we are going to get through this trip, we have got to be open and honest, isn't that what we agreed? You have to tell me why you got angry."

Fred put his head down and hung his arms over his knees as he said, "Bob told me that Sheila had told him about what you had told her."

I turned around and faced him, knee to knee and asked him, keeping my eyes to his, "Just what exactly did Sheila tell Bob?"

Fred fidgeted somewhat under my gaze until I whispered, "Tell me, Freddy."

Then he blurted out, "Why did you have to tell them for? It is none of their business!"

I had known it was a mistake the second I had said that to Sheila.

I put my head down and said, "She put the baby in my arms and I was just so torn inside... and then she asked if I was expecting again... the next thing I knew I was giving the baby back to her as quick as I could and telling her that we have only been like brother and sister and it would take time."

In English, I added, "I'm so sorry."

He suddenly focussed his eyes on me and said, "You know, that is the first time since I have known you, that you actually said 'I'm sorry.' But, you shouldn't need to be sorry about anything. The rule is to think before you speak or act, that way there is no need to say you're sorry. Has it ever occurred to you why we don't have the words 'I'm sorry' in our language? There are no such words in Ojibway."

I kept my head down. I didn't know what else to say. Somewhere deep inside, a resentment began to build. He didn't need to lecture to me, I knew these things as well as he did! I also had his share of "I'm sorry!" How dare he lecture me on who says I'm sorry!

As the silence lengthened, I asked, "Why did you find my comment so upsetting? Why were you so mad that they found out?"

He turned and glared at me, then softly said, "No, I am not the cause of the problem here, you are the one with the problem."

I looked down and thought that perhaps he was right. Maybe I was indeed the one with the problem. Wasn't I the one that always made sure that things were always at the proper distance? The one that always remembered things had got close enough? It was almost a daily challenge that if he could keep his distance then so would I! But, it wasn't really that. My problem lay plainly in the fact that I did not want to have another baby. I did not want to get pregnant again while things were the way they were.

His hand moved and it closed over mine.

He held my hand as he looked at me and whispered, "Why? Why did you have to tell them that?"

I looked up into Freddy's eyes and said, "Because I didn't want to feel like I was the failure... that I couldn't have another child."

I watched his eyes travel all along the shoreline before he said, "That comment from Bob made me feel like I was less of a man because I couldn't even give you another child."

I couldn't meet his eyes. I knew he was looking at me. Oh, how sorry I was for ever opening my mouth to that woman! I looked at the lake and on a sudden impulse, I got up and dove into the water. Its silence and intense pressure held me in its murky depths. I held my breath for the longest time ever.

When I came up for air, I felt Fred's arms close around me in the water. He held me so tight, that I could barely turn around to look at him at which time, I felt his urgent lips on mine. There was a sudden overwhelming pressure that seemed to engulf us both as we got out of the water and gauged each other wearily. There were no tricks here, no one was going to back down at the last minute. We got back to the cabin and no sooner had the door closed that I heard the lock click into place when I felt Fred's arms around me. Supper would wait. That night, I discovered a depth of love that I had never experienced in my whole life.

At the store the next day, I was walking behind Fred and he had gone in ahead when I heard a high whistle and there I saw Ron sitting on the platform by the storage shed. I turned from the door and walked toward him. He sat there with his head a bit to the side. I felt his eyes travel up and down my whole body. I could not ever remember noticing this about him before. When did he start doing this to me? I became rather uncomfortable and embarrassed by the time I reached him.

I came to a stop in front of him and asked, "What? Why are you looking at me like that?"

He smiled and answered rather softly, "You are so beautiful. No, you are gorgeous! You can't tell me that you are not aware of what you look like!"

My mouth flew open, trying to think of something to say when I noticed his eyes focussing on someone behind me. I turned to see Fred standing at the store door, waiting for me.

Ron whispered just loud enough for me to hear, "See, he's not even going to let you out of his sight for a second now."

I smiled slightly. I couldn't think of a thing to say, so I turned around quickly and headed back to the store. I could not figure out what had come over Ron! Never had he done that before! Was he just trying to aggravate Fred? But, why?

We went into the store and Fred went right through and into the back mail room. I stood around in the open store area when I started to feel my skin crawl! From what source? Then I turned and saw Ted sitting there in the corner of the store room. An old battered green cap sat on top his dirty, long unkempt hair that trailed over his grey leathery looking face. From between the strands of hair, I saw the beady eyes glaring at me.

A pink tongue shot out several times, sweeping the length of his thin lips before I heard him say in a rasping voice, "My good Charlie... watch for those... you think... who care."

I smiled and nodded in his direction. Oh, he looked bad! He looked like someone from a horror movie! He couldn't be much older than the rest of us here, we all played together as children. I looked back at Ted one more time and went into the mail room.

After we sorted through the mail, Fred found out how much the sales of the fur were and how much we owed. We came out in the financial shape we thought we would. There were several hundred dollars that I could not account for when I glanced at the balance sheet but I did not question him. I knew he did not know how much I could discern with a glance. It was none of my business and I had no doubt he knew exactly what he was doing.

I ran to Mother's cabin before the train came to find the Groundhogs laying sprawled out on the floor, up on their elbows, head to head. I looked over Lenny's shoulder to see a whole bunch of wingless house-flies, frantically circling a deep ceramic bowl which sat between the two boys.

I gasped, whispering, "Oh, my gosh! You are not supposed to do that! Better kill them quick! Better pray they don't get back at you because that is exactly what you or your loved ones will become."

Something in my voice got Lenny quickly on his feet and he began a weird dance as he stomped on the flies, just missing his brother's hands as Benny scrambled up.

Mother and O had apparently gone fishing. Flies forgotten, the boys scrambled up and followed me back to the station where Fred was waiting. In that time, they talked non-stop.

Between lapses of tuning-out, Benny caught my attention as he was saying, "...the cabin was dark, but we saw someone sneaking around behind the cabin and then Lenny tripped and the man saw us... I think. Then we thought he was chasing us so we ran into the bushes toward the swamp and then..."

I interrupted, "Where? Who was sneaking around?"

Lenny answered, "Your place. We heard you came back so we were coming to visit you but the cabin was dark. That's when we saw the guy sneaking around behind your cabin."

A shock went through me as the information sank in, but Benny was babbling on again, "Anyway, Lenny tripped over a huge stump and suddenly, it popped up shining bright! I screamed and crashed into it, a chunk fell on my pants and I grabbed some. Did you know old stumps shine in the night, Janine? Huh? When we got home, we looked at the shining piece in my hand and it was dark bluish green."

I answered, "Yes. Yes, I remember seeing one when I was a kid. But, they don't shine long do they?"

Someone responded with an, "Oh."

I wondered if it had been the Weesquachak sneaking around again. Who was this Weesquachak anyway? Fred's invisible man. I wonder who it will turn out to be if, or when, he catches him. But then, how on earth would he know we were here? The boys must be mistaken! They could have seen a dog.

Fred did not drink and he never left my side during the entire time we were in the village, or on the shopping trip to Savant Lake. I mentioned the man the boys had said they saw. He thought a moment but then shrugged. We said nothing more about it.

I told him the story about Sheila and her baby and that Nisha guy. He just threw his head back and laughed out loud. We talked of other things all the way to Savant Lake on the train and back again.

I smiled to myself when I remembered us at the store in Savant Lake, how Fred stopped at the newspaper and magazine rack and with a glance, indicated that I shouldn't forget to get them. I shook my head. I felt no need to try to keep track of what was happening around the world. I was only interested in what was happening with my life and those around me. As for magazines, I didn't care much for make-up or fashions. My jeans and checkered shirt were good enough for me at this time.

I laughed at the stories Fred told me on the train. He talked of many things he had seen and done in the communities along the railroad tracks. It reminded me of Nisha. I still could not believe that the spying man could have been Nisha. Where was he? No one had seen him since the spring after Sheila's story. I listened to Fred. They were stories of how his buddies got their nicknames. There was one he told of a guy named Tom who came around the corner of a deck they were replacing. He was just about to call to Bill that there was a phone call for him—just as Bill hit the last board off the frame, the board came flying and whacked Tom right across the face and broke his nose! Tom got the name Board Nose.

Then there was another time when they were replacing the roof at Ed's house. Ed was below, reaching down to pick his tool belt up off the ground when Andy, on the roof, knocked a can of roofing nails over and they rained down on top of Ed's head. He had little bloody specks all over his neck and back. They'd sing, "Nails keep falling on my head," whenever they saw him.

Then there was Jerry and the wet cement mixed in a wheel barrow all ready for the fence posts they were putting in. Jerry tripped on a board and staggered backwards and slowly sank into the wheel barrow—sat right down into the wet cement! He got up amidst howls of laughter and went inside the house to change. Later when his wife got home, she found his jeans sitting upright on top the laundry basket. He became known as Hard Ass.

Fred had stories for each of the train stops where we watched people getting on and off the train. He would point out buildings and land sites telling me what had happened here and there. I began to know and understand a side of Fred that I had had no idea of up until now, including the people who stopped to say hello, who shook his hand and wished us well. It felt good to be with him.

One thing that I found to my dismay was that I had only one month's supply of birth-control pills left. They had been stuck in the corner of my suitcase. After I had lost the baby, I made sure I had them with me at all times. What had happened in the cabin would be all right since I was only a day to having my periods, but then I couldn't be sure either. The pills I had left, I took with me back to the bush. There had just been no way I could get to a drug store. Fred only shopped in Savant Lake now where there wasn't a drug store. I wanted to go to Sioux Lookout where there was one, but Fred insisted we could get what we needed in Savant Lake. I could not bring myself to tell him why I wanted to go to Sioux Lookout. Knowing that I had at least one month of worry-free days, I followed Fred contentedly back to our cabin at Clay Lake.

* * * *

Fred's mind wandered as he paddled along the long stretch of Smoothrock Lake. It wasn't that he was unfeeling, he had felt the pain that she went through. The year before, alone on a snow machine ride, she had struggled while her body strained to push the dead baby out of her. He had cried with her each mile of the way. He could tell each time he felt the anguished clasp tighten around his middle. How could he not feel that! It was only when the sun was coming up, that the tension lessened and he was able to disentangle her hands from his jacket. He had stretched himself out on the snow in an effort to show her that life would begin anew between her and himself in the dawn of this coming new day. He'd had such a strong urge to bury his face into her arms, to hug her, and tell her how much he loved her. But, the deal remained that she would be at her corner and he in his. Even with this arrangement, he had been satisfied. It had been better than none.

He had hoped with time, that she would change her mind and that they would renegotiate. But, oh, she was one stubborn person! Not once did she waver, and it got to a point where he was calling himself every name under the sun and kicking himself until he could not even face his shaving mirror! Right from the moment they had walked into the cabin at the trap-line that afternoon, he knew things would be very different when she immediately snatched her aprons from the kitchen table and threw them into a box and grabbed the chisel. Oh, he had loved her more than he ever had at that very moment! Then came the painful weeks, one after the other.

But now, at the last portage, he watched her as she stooped down at the water's edge to splash water on her face. He remembered her comment about the white water-lilies and he was tempted to comment that she herself, was now pure nature and wonderfully natural and that nature could never be duplicated! He looked to her as the source of oxygen for his lungs and blood for his heart. He loved her wholly and utterly and he knew he would have to adjust to the influence of others between them. He looked on his love for her as a sort of self-preservation that he should try to protect at all costs, that which kept him alive and well. And, that was the extent of his love for Charlie.

Looking back, he was grateful that the anger that sparked between them about the comments from Bob and Sheila seemed to light the most incredible flame that finally engulfed them that night in the cabin at the village. But then, Weesquachak had also been there. When they got off the train that evening, he had found himself scanning the faces, trying to figure out which of the men was Weesquachak because he was not absolutely sure it was Nisha. Nisha was not in the community at the moment. It had to be someone from this community, if, that had been a person last night. He saw Ted, Ron and about four other guys at the storage shack beside the store. There was no way it could have been any of them. He knew them too well.

CHAPTER 21

There was such a release of tension. Fun was more spontaneous, as was the loving gestures and touches. We revelled in abandonment for the entire month. I knew that I had to break the news to Fred after July because then, I would not have any birth-control pills left. I knew that this was not fair to Freddy as I prepared myself for the separation that would be required for the time that I did not have the pills.

During the second week of August, Jason, the guide at the tourist camp, started coming by to visit every once in a while. One time, Fred had gone to check the fish net when Jason arrived, so I asked him when the next plane was coming in. I made no bones about the situation and that I needed to go to a drug store for some pills. He understood and he promised me that he would come to pick me up in the morning before the plane came.

Then he started telling me about the tourist who got a hook caught on the seat of his pants. When they had cut his pants out around the hook, they found that the hook was firmly imbedded on his left buttock. This sent me laughing out loud. I could just imagine this bald headed top executive of some company in the States being in that position! It was at that point that Fred came around the corner of the cabin. He came in to find Jason inside the cabin with both of us doubled over in laughter. Fred reacted in a fashion that reflected a man being made a fool of; who was being laughed at by his wife and her lover! He just turned around and walked out again, totally consumed in rage! I was embarrassed. Jason left after a while and I went about getting ready for bed.

I was furious that Fred would do that. When was he going to learn to be civil when other people were around. I hated his jealousy! It was quite late at night and I was beginning to worry as to where he could have gone to when I heard him coming in and then he went straight to bed. I got up and lit the lamp and sat down beside the single bed where he lay.

He gave no response so I pulled his arm and demanded, "Talk! We must talk! We must talk or... we can't go on like this. We must talk because we're going back to exactly what we were doing the first time! Do you remember that?"

Fred sat up on the bed, moved to the bench but then stood up and paced the floor before he flopped back down on the bench saying, "Talk? Why don't you tell me what you're thinking! I can see what you're feeling but I don't know what you're thinking! Everyday, you tell me that you love me but then, you don't love me. Sometimes I find you wanting me but you won't let me near you... sometimes you are telling me you don't want me, yet you love me, at other times, you don't love me... gull darn it, woman! Tell me what is going on with you?"

I took a deep breath, and put my head down before I gathered the nerve to begin, "I only had one month's supply of birth-control pills. Then I saw you with the cradle board we had made for Baby..."

I swallowed, trying to keep my voice even as I fought the tears that rolled down my cheeks and continued, "I was terrified that I would get pregnant again. I still feel the pain so bad. That day when I saw you with that cradle in the storage shed I ran because I had to have a good cry. I'm sorry. I didn't want you to see me like that. I'm not ready yet, for another baby."

I went to him to put my arms around him. I so desperately needed a hug. He pushed me away and I sat stunned and quiet beside the bench for the longest time. He lay back down on the single bed and turned his back to me. After a while, I got up and got back into bed. I lay looking into the darkness. There was only one way I could see out of this situation. It was for me to get those pills, come back, and everything would be alright again.

The next morning he was gone before I got up. I heard the boat taking off from the dock. It was the same thing over again as he had done the first year we were together. So, I got up and got ready for Jason. Soon, he arrived to get me and when the plane came in a short while later, I left on the plane that morning. I arrived at Sioux Lookout that night. I went to bed early and the next morning, I made a visit to the bank and then went to the drug store as soon as I could. I caught the afternoon train back to Armstrong and was at the dock the very next day. When I got off the plane at the tourist camp at Clay Lake, Jason came up to me in a very sheepish manner, like he had done something wrong

I asked, "What's wrong?"

Jason never said a word but just pointed at Fred's boat on the beach. I knew then that Jason was just telling me that Fred had left. I nodded and got into the boat and headed back to the cabin.

When I arrived, I found the cabin empty, much as I had left it. According to the schedule, I knew it would be another week before the plane came back with a new load of tourists. I decided to take the canoe back to the village. I had to find him quick. I did not trust him alone out there. It would be a three day trip at the most and as soon as I got over the rapids between Clay Lake and Whitewater Lake, I would be on my way.

As it happened, it was a good two days later when I finally came out of the Whitewater Lake channel. I paddled very slowly and softly for I soon discovered that there were people ahead of me. I had come across a campfire that had been doused but was left with underground moss fire smoldering at the Clay River portage. When I paddled out of the channel and out into the open of Whitewater Lake, I discovered six canoes in front of me. As soon as they saw me, they stopped. I watched their canoes drifting and waiting for me until I came abreast to them.

In the evening stillness, I heard one of the women saying, "Who do you think that could be? Oh, he's a man for sure."

Another snickered and said, "What would a woman be doing around here in the middle of nowhere?"

Another said, "No, wait, I see a pony-tail behind that baseball cap. Must be an Indian woman, no white woman would be around here by herself!"

Another said, "Eh, look, the canoe is coming on in one straight line, no left or right swerve with each of her strokes, some kind of professional!"

"Hey, got that cream for blisters handy?"

"Oh, just to hear his voice at this moment... one more word, and I'll shower embers over your sleeping bag! You hear me?"

They chuckled. It seemed that they were playing scenes from a movie or something.

As I got closer I lay my paddle across the canoe, leaned back and said, "It is such a quiet evening, I'd be able to carry on a conversation with you from clear across the lake."

The canoe carried me right between their three canoes on each side. They looked at me and I examined their state and decided that they were no worse off than what I'd be before we got to the village. I had guessed that they had started from Nakina and I was right.

One woman wanted to know what a white woman was doing in this area since I had no Indian accent whatsoever.

I pulled up my sleeve and said, "I'm afraid this is as light as I get."

The others laughed when they must have realized that I was only a few shades lighter than my early spring and summer tan.

I wondered just what they were expecting Indian accent would sound like, so I said, "Well, I doon'no watch'yu'wanna'see bu'looks to me, I cun'teech yu more, if yu cun cutch up wi' me!"

In one stroke of my paddle I shot well away from them. Some giggles and hoots followed. They followed me stroke for stroke down the length of Whitewater Lake to Best Island. I pulled up to a stop at the long finger of sand. A deep sorrow assailed me at this point. How many times had I ran along this beach over the years, screeching, howling, and screaming in excitement and happiness. And just last month, I had laughed hard when Fred discovered a little black bloodsucker stuck between his toes when we were in bed. Good thing he was wrapped inside his own blanket. Now, I was coming upon this stretch of sand with heaviness in my chest and a dozen strangers behind me. I continued past the island and through the channel and into the quiet bay toward the portage.

The ladies. Oh, I found that they were a motley crew, full of energy, confidence, and a good bit of strange camping habits. I named them all in my mind as I watched and observed them. The quiet, stone-faced one, I called the Sentry. The one that had her legs over the front of the canoe wiggling her toes and then sat before the fire wiggling her toes became Mrs. Wiggles. There was Ms. Winks, who winked as if to indicate that she knew something that the others didn't. Then there was the Sergeant, who liked to bellow authoritative commands as to exactly where each tent was to be pitched. There was Corrinna, C-o-r-r-i-n-n-a as she spelled it at her introduction, as if it made any difference what she was called out here amongst the mosquitoes and the frogs! And then, there was the Trapper. One glance told me that she was quite comfortable in the bush. She didn't hesitate to do what needed doing and she did it very quickly and efficiently. I remember thinking at one point that I would like to spend some time with her at the trap-line. We'd probably catch more animals, the two of us together than... I let the thought go.

All the other younger women seemed to just take the orders and go about the motions of getting through the day. It reminded me of office procedures. As we were going through portage number three, past Whitewater Lake into Smoothrock Lake, one of the younger troupe, Miss Mouse, lost a shoe in the mud and was softly whimpering and gasping to herself with distaste as she kept hesitantly dipping her toe and her heel on each side of her submerged sucked-up-in-the-mud shoe.

I glanced at her as I walked by and said, "Just make sure there are no slugs sticking to your sock when you put that shoe back on."

I continued with my canoe on my shoulders.

When we came out into Smoothrock Lake, the women took a dip at the beach. Some took off running along the beach with just their panties on.

"Hey!" I yelled, "Watch out for broken glass!"

The Sentry asked behind me, "What glass? We're in the middle of nowhere."

I turned and smiled, "You saw that campfire site, it's a good place for shore-lunch for the tourists and I'd bet my life that there are broken bottles all along the shoreline."

Suddenly there was a shout, "There! There's another one!"

The Trapper had disappeared in the opposite direction of the sand beach. I walked along the shore until I had left them all behind me. Close to an overhanging tree with its branches scraping the surface of water, I came across two more ladies out in the water. I lay down on my back and watched the clouds drifting by overhead.

Soon, Wiggles came out of the water and sat down beside me, saying, "Oh, I'm glad there is such a thing as tampons!"

I heard Ms. Simpleton coming up right behind Wiggles saying that she was all for trying to catch a loon just in case it had a fish in it. Ms. Simpleton came and lay down rather close beside me.

I stretched out and yawned and said, "You know, my mother used to tell us that since blood-suckers are naturally attracted to blood, they would all wriggle their way into your vagina to suck up the blood. That's why we were never allowed to go swimming if we were on our periods."

Suddenly, Simpleton sat bolt upright and ran like the dickens, spraying sand into our faces.

I lifted my head and looked at Wiggles, "What's up with her?"

Wiggles giggled and looked up at the clouds beside me before she said, "She doesn't wear tampons. She wears pads and puts nothing on when she goes swimming."

I was seized with the giggles but brought them under control as the Sentry came walking by. She was collecting all the broken pieces of beer bottles she could find as if she were getting a hundred dollars a piece.

The clouds coming up above the treetops looked menacing. A hurried conference ensued at the beach as I pushed my canoe out. I was a good way out before I heard the ladies thumping their canoes, coming up behind me. They had decided to come with me. I did not relish getting stuck at this end of the lake if the waves got too high. We were about half way across the lake when the storm hit. We hugged the inside shores of the islands as the rain came down in sheets. After blowing pretty much the rest of the way, we finally entered the narrow channel to the portage at the other end of the lake. I was totally drenched although I had a raincoat on. The ladies were in much the same shape as I led them to the portage camp-site.

After I set up my tent, I stood by the lake beside the overturned canoes and watched a white mist coming up like smoke from the lake as the thick drizzle came down in sheets creating a constant sound like sizzling bacon in a frying pan. Then, from out of the mist flew a sea-gull, gliding in the rain-swept winds, right toward me. Then it suddenly swerved up and disappeared over the treetops. I turned to see Miss Mouse behind me, with her head also turned to where the sea-gull had disappeared. She had a big smile on her face.

At the Smoothrock Lake portage the next morning, we were all dressed and I was waiting to see how they were going to start the fire, when, in a rather loud voice, Simpleton demanded that the Indian show the troupe how to start the morning fire on such a damp wet and miserable morning like this! I knew she was trying to pay me back for her panic on the beach the evening before. They all turned to me with smiles. So, without comment, I went to my canoe and got out my little jug of a Javex container and pulled out my plastic bag of pine branches and twigs, and headed to the campfire site.

I saw now that the comment had brought out the whole crew to see how an Indian was going to start a fire after the storm we had. I went to a small dry poplar tree to the side of the portage landing and pushed it down, quickly chopping it into three-foot lengths. I then shoved the contents of the plastic bag underneath. I piled on the limbs and chunks from the tree, grabbed the little Javex container and poured some of the gasoline from it and threw a match to the wood. I had a big roaring fire going in two minutes flat! The ladies started laughing and clapping. The Trapper with her blond hair looking like it had just been struck with lightning, stood to the side with a grin on her face, but she made no comment. I smiled. When you live in the bush, you learn to use the most practical and efficient means of getting things done. It could likely mean the difference between life and death.

We entered the lake to the village late in the evening. The women all paddled to the vacant field site beside the dock. The Sentry and Mrs. Wiggles were sent to call the train dispatcher to notify the train that the scheduled half-dozen canoes had arrived on time.

I saw the Groundhogs arrive on the women's second trip back from the station. My arms absently went around them, but they were stiff and unresponsive and I realized that they were now beyond the age for hugs, especially in front of strange ladies.

I asked them, "How's Mom?"

They both answered, "She's fine. She's with Dad at home."

I had just noticed that they were now almost the same height as I was. When we were well away from the others, I hugged them both to me as we made our way to my canoe. Lenny got on at the front with the paddle, Benny got on in the middle without a paddle, and I pushed the canoe off and we headed out into the dark waters.

The sun had gone down long ago and it was getting dark quickly. Like seasoned hunters, the boys insisted we sneak up on the cabin. We got the canoe to Mother's landing without any noise until we pulled it up on the rocky shore. Somehow we knocked Lenny over and he landed with a loud splash into the water, followed with some loud curses! With all that racket, their father appeared at the door. He stood there shadowed with the lamplight around him. I wondered what he was thinking. He looked miserable. I wished I hadn't come here first. Maybe I should have gone to Fred's cabin. I left the packsack and everything inside the canoe and entered the cabin behind the boys.

Mother was on the bed, propped up on pillows and O was sitting at the table.

He asked, "So, how did you get into town?"

"With the women in the canoes," I answered.

I sat down at the foot of their double bed rubbing Mother's toes, massaging them, trying to make an effort to connect with her somehow before his voice came again, "They all got on the train then?"

Mother answered, "Oh, shucks! You just missed a whole bunch of white women, and how they would have loved to have gotten their hands on you."

A quick action from the table sent a dishcloth across Mother's face and she giggled as she made a face at him. O indicated a pot on the stove and I dished out a bowl of meat and macaroni soup. He was now lying on the bed and I sat down at the table and told them about The Sentry, Simpleton, Miss Mouse, Winks, the Trapper and Mrs. Wiggles. They laughed at my descriptions of each. I finished eating and washed the bowl. Then, I sat there a moment watching them. They seemed happy. O was actually smiling and laughing quite a bit now.

After a moment, I turned to the boys and asked, "Is Fred in the community?"

There was a silence for a full minute before Lenny said, "Yeah. He got off the train this morning but he was still drunk this afternoon."

This was it then. It was over. I sat there looking at my feet then decided that I was going to go to the cabin. I wanted my suitcases from there. If I didn't get them now, he would be here at Mother's place when he heard I was here. Without a word, I stood up and went out. I pushed the canoe back into the water and paddled out into the open lake. I felt safer out here and I'd get there quicker.

I paddled in the darkness and listened to the sounds of the community. Everything was loud and clear. I even heard the door close at Mother's cabin. Then I heard the boys laughing and giggling. They were probably wrestling on the way to the outhouse. I reached the other end of the shore and slowly maneuvered the canoe past the solid black point where Fred and I first went swimming together. Then into the dark currents of the creek. I could barely make out the outline of the rocks through the small channel before I reached the little bay where the landing was. I pulled the canoe up and heaved the packsack over my shoulder and pulled my sleeping bag up on top and threw the light tent over the top of everything else. I smiled as I made my way to Fred's cabin. I must look like a real trapper just returning home. I wondered if he was home. I doubted it, he was probably at Karen's place! I paused to check the door to see if it was locked from the inside but the door opened at my push. He was not here. What did I expect anyway? He had gone back to drinking and back to Karen!

I entered and deposited my packsack, bags, and the rest of the things behind the door and lit a match. The match light found the table and I lit the coal-oil lamp. At that instant, I saw Fred turn around on the bed and his face registered surprise and then I saw Karen fast asleep beside him! I stood there stock-still for a full minute before I whirled around and ran back down the path toward the lake. I felt my face totally awash with tears as I pushed the canoe back into the water. I headed out into the lake as fast as I could. How could he do this to me! Why? Oh, I loved him so much! Why, did he do this? I really thought he loved me! After I had remained adrift for a good five minutes, I paddled with quick strokes and then slowly drifted past the island and made for the main east shoreline toward Mother's place.

I was just coming around the corner of the island when I heard a shout from shore, "Charlie! Charlie! Come over here!"

It was Fred! He was following me on the path along the shore! I drifted along until I reached the point across from Mother's place. I couldn't go to Mother's, he'd make a big scene and upset everybody. I steered the canoe to the point, got out, and pulled the canoe up. Sure enough, I could hear him coming up over the rocks and into the stand of trees before he emerged behind me. I sat there with my elbows on my knees, waiting for the on-slaught. He was drunk but not staggering. He must have slept it off some.

"How did you get here? Where did you go when you took off? Eh? Who do you think you are anyway, walking into my cabin like that! You still think you're so high and mighty don't you? Say something!"

I stood up in front of him and said in a low voice, "You just remember that everybody in the whole community can hear you. You are asking me what I was doing there? What were you doing in bed with that woman? Huh?"

I felt spit spraying on my face as he hissed at me, "You asked for that! You are the one who's always pushing me away. I'm only human you know. You always turn your back on me. I am not good enough for you, is that it?"

I hissed back, barely above a whisper, "I went out to get some birth-control pills. I did not want to get pregnant! I don't want a baby right now. Do you understand? Because you would only take off on me again, wouldn't you? Wouldn't you? That's why I left, but I came back again when I said I would, but you were gone! Why did you leave? Huh? Why did you leave?"

He turned to the lake now as he said, "I didn't think you were coming back. I thought maybe you left with Jason. He wasn't there either. Did you consider having his baby instead of mine?"

I heard myself say, "What? Jason? Why on earth would I leave with Jason? Listen to yourself will you? I love you and only you! But what about you? Eh? What about you and that woman! Why did you go and do that to me for! Just how many children does she have of yours? Eh?"

"Two! The two young ones are mine!"

His words hit me with such a jolt I nearly doubled over in pain as he yelled at me. I heard a moan escape my throat and then I pushed him away from me so hard I heard him splash into the water. He was swearing a blue streak and I could hear water dripping off him before I could get my shaking legs back into the canoe. I pushed the canoe away and paddled out into the middle of the lake. I could feel my hot tears streaming over my face as I paddled hard. Then I heard a motor starting and it was coming toward me at full speed! Could he see me? I paddled faster, trying to get to the island. I could tell he was on a big aluminum boat with a twenty-horse motor! It came straight at me, coming very close as I swung my canoe around. It roared past and turned around again. It was Fred alright. He must have just jumped into the first boat he saw.

He slowed down beside me yelling, "Get in the boat! You hear me? Nobody! Nobody else will ever touch you. Do you hear me? Get in the boat!"

I yelled back, "No! Go away! Get away from me!"

I paddled away as hard as I could. The boat rared full speed and came straight at me. With a bang, it hit the front of the canoe. My paddle went flying and I was spun around so quickly I nearly overturned. He still screamed at me to get into the boat.

Suddenly, I was aware of the noise of another motor and the sound of another boat approaching at full speed. It intercepted Fred and there was a lot of shouting and banging between the boats. A large bright flashlight was swinging back and forth and I saw a man jumping into Fred's boat. It was John. It must have been John's boat that Fred was in. John was Ron's next door neighbour. Ron! He was now pulling my canoe alongside his boat. He pulled me into the boat and tied the canoe behind the motor. John's motor started and took off for shore. Ron kept his arm around me as he slowly headed for Mother's landing.

I sat there shaking and then a pain slowly started to increase around my chest. I could barely breathe when we finally arrived at Mother's place. I went up to the cabin, bent over, gasping for breath and moaning from the pain that had clamped itself around my chest. Mother was beside me and she ushered me to the single bed beside the window. I sat there bent over as she pressed a hot cup of tea into my hands. I watched O and Ron enter the cabin. I felt very embarrassed that Ron got involved in all this.

Then O was in front of me saying, "So, you created some entertainment for the community, did you?"

Suddenly, Mother was there pushing him aside saying, "I'll give them a bit more with you at the end of my walking stick if you don't keep your mouth shut!"

I was aware that Ron was still in the room. When I felt the pressure clamp of tension begin to release my chest, I looked up to find Ron standing beside the stove. His eyes met mine and he stood unmoving. I couldn't tell what was going through his mind but he slowly smiled and a twinkle came into his eyes.

I was seized with an incredible urge to laugh and I started giggling. Soon my giggles turned into outright laughter as I bent over with my arms around my waist. I realized that no one else was laughing and Mother was laying me down on the bed wiping my face with a wet cloth.

When I woke, all was still. Ron was gone. I could hear the boys breathing, asleep on their double bed in the corner. O was snoring slightly in the next room. I could never hear Mother's soft breathing in her sleep. I lay awake crying and wondering how I was going to deal with all this. Although I was aware that there was the possibility of him doing something like this again, I never believed he would do this to me again! What did he see in that married woman! In fact, until I saw them in bed with my own eyes, I would have never believed it possible! I really truly relieved that he loved me! He would never have done this if he loved me! I felt betrayed, thrown aside, and I was angry. After all we had gone through in getting through the communication barriers, beliefs, and expectations, we were right back where we started! There was no more room in my heart to carry this and go on. I wanted it to stop. I would have to leave and never come back.

Oh, being a woman can have its perks too. Especially when this stupid man didn't even know I was there! Ha, ha,ha,ha... Oh, my poor little lost one! Hah, I found out my shifting form didn't take to moving from man to raven too often. Kind of skidded my brain on the surface too much. That's why my echo...

CHAPTER 22

The next morning, Mother and O decided to set the fish net. They left right after breakfast. The sun was shining and the sky was clear blue. I felt a wrench in my heart. I wished Fred and I were instantly set back in time to July when we stood by the shore beside the boat deciding how we were going to spend such a beautiful day. At this point, I didn't think the birth-control pills were worth it! I had lost everything I worked so hard for to make this relationship work. Just because I did not want to get pregnant... And, all he wanted was for me to show him how much I loved him by giving him a baby. But, there was no turning back.

As I went about washing the dishes and sweeping the floor, I realized that I kept glancing out the window or pausing by the door to look down the path. I was expecting Fred to come and talk. I heard the train arrive and pull out again. Then, silence descended on me.

After I cleaned up the cabin, I went down to the lake and sat down on a rock and watched the tiny minnows swim by.

Sometime later, I heard footsteps coming up behind me and I steeled myself for the encounter. How would he be, angry? Sorry? I turned, but it was only Ron. He sat down on a rock next to me and did not say a thing for the longest time. I waited.

After about five minutes, he said, "He got on the train this morning."

I looked across the bay to the point where I had pushed Fred into the water last night. How could he just leave me like this! He couldn't even be bothered to come over to talk to me, to my face, to tell me he wanted nothing more to do with me, ever again.

I heaved a big sigh. So, it was up to me again, and me alone.

After a while, I turned to Ron and said, "Thanks for last night."

He threw a twig into the water and I watched it move away, as he said, "I've told you many times, I'm always here for you."

I smiled and looked down into the water again. Yes, he always said that.

Then he reached and brushed a strand of hair away from my face and said, "So, what are you going to do now. He won't be back for a long time. Why don't you stay here for the rest of the summer? We could go fishing."

I shook my head, saying, "I can't stay here. He'll be back and it will start all over again. I have to leave."

Then, his voice came softly, "I could make sure he never bothers you again."

My head came up and his eyes held mine as shock went through me, for I saw no trace of gentle Ron in those deep brown eyes. I was looking into the eyes of... I looked away shaking my head, thinking, this is crazy! I'm just over exhausted.

When I looked at him again, he was looking out into the shimmering lake.

I asked, "What do you mean you could make sure he never bothers me again? I don't want you getting involved between us. This is our problem, my problem. Stay away from him."

Instantly, he turned to me and gently said, "I didn't mean to upset you. I wouldn't hurt him. Huh! Me hurt him? He'd probably wrap my hide around his fists! I was only saying that if, maybe if you were with me or made it look like that, he wouldn't bother you."

I smiled. That was nice of him to say so. He was always nice. He was always trying to be helpful.

I turned to him as a thought occurred to me, "By the way, why are you always saying those things to me. You do have a wife don't you? I always thought you were just being a gentleman and being as comforting and gentle as you could be, to make others feel better. I mean, you always have, but I'm not so sure these days. I'm just never sure anymore if you're for real or whether you're just joking to make me laugh."

He kept his head down for the longest time. I was beginning to think that I may have hurt him bad if he had actually been serious about his suggestion.

But then, he looked at me with a grin creeping into his face.

I smiled. He was just trying to make me feel better.

I thought a bit about where I should go and said, "I can't stay here. After last night, I can just imagine what everyone's saying. I don't want them watching me, talking about me or feeling sorry for me. I'll leave on the evening train. I'm just not sure where to go. It's like I have so many choices, I don't know which one to pick."

He knew I was joking with the last comment. A sad smile played on his lips but he didn't answer me. I could see the flash of paddles now. Mother and O were returning.

That evening, I said goodbye to Mother and O before I set out in the canoe to Fred's cabin. I was returning the canoe to his boat landing and there I would pick up my suitcases from his cabin and I would be gone. This time, I knew I was not coming back. Nothing could mend what had happened.

The Groundhogs had taken off after supper and never returned. They were probably at the train station already. I was hoping that they would help me with my suitcases. I got to the landing and was pulling the canoe up when I heard someone coming down the path to the lake. Who could that be? Not Fred! But it was Ron. He came and took the other side of the canoe. We pulled it up and turned it over. Without a word he followed me up the path to the cabin door.

I expected the door to be locked but it swung open when I pushed it. It was very dark inside. Ron struck a match behind me and lit the candle while I picked up my suitcases. They were exactly where I had left them. I had nothing else to take. Without a word, I blew out the light and turned to follow Ron out the door when I felt his hands gripping me firmly on the arms. I froze. I did not move as he pulled me against his body. He held me so tightly that I was barely able to breathe before I dropped my suitcases and started to push his shoulders away.

I heard him whisper against my ear, "c.b.t.m. Janine!"

His breath was warm against my cheek and I pushed him away.

"Please, don't do that."

Suddenly he stopped dead still. Then slowly he pulled my head to his shoulder and there he gently ran his hand over my head and over my shoulders.

He said, "Oh, baby, I'm sorry. I didn't mean to scare you. You say you're leaving for good. I may not see you again... in a long time and... it's just that I have loved you for so long and I could never reach you. I have tried to love other women, but I can't! I keep loving only you. I have always loved only you. But, I know you can not love me, I know. You have told me that over and over again since we were kids... but I just want you to know that I will always love you anyway... can you understand that? That's what I have been trying to tell you! Don't be afraid of me, I am only here to love you. My whole life's purpose is to do anything I can to help you!"

I had to get out of there right that minute! This was not the Ron I knew!

I said in a rather loud voice, "Shhhh, here they come. I sent the boys to meet me here. Now, I'll have to tell them I got lost in the dark inside the cabin and kept bumping into you. Come on, let's go."

He released me and then was out the door. I picked up the suitcases and went out. He was standing in the clearing waiting for me.

He came toward me slowly to take my suitcases as he said, "There is no one out here, Janine."

I glanced around thinking of course not. I did not tell the boys to meet me here.

As gently as I could, I said, "Ron, it's okay. I will carry them. I don't want them, I mean the whole community, saying things about you and me that are not true. And they will gossip if you are seen carrying my bags from Fred's cabin. Thank you for all your help. Thank you for making me laugh. Thanks for being there when I needed someone. Take care and go back to your wife and be happy."

His hand came up and gently brushed my cheek but he said nothing as he turned and disappeared down the path to the lake. I walked toward the railway station. As soon as I came into the light of the store windows, the Groundhogs descended on me, running at full speed. They grabbed my suitcases but then walked very sedately, like a procession behind the Queen, all the way to the train station. I giggled. That was our last fun. When I'm gone, they would practice how they had walked to the train station.

As I boarded the train, I knew there was a chance that Fred could be on it, so I very cautiously went down the aisle before I found a seat where I thought I could sit as inconspicuously as possible. I had just paid for the train fare to Sioux Lookout when Gook came up from behind and sat down beside me. It was such a wonderful surprise! She took my hand without a word and we sat there for a long time.

I could not think of a thing to say to her.

Then, I smiled and asked, "So where are you off to?"

She glanced at me and said, "Oh, Remy got sick when she was supposed to bring him down, so now I have to go get him because she's gone already."

So, Remy's annual summer visit was a bit late this year.

Then she asked, "Where are you off to?"

I said, "Sioux Lookout. I'm going to see how much money I have left at the bank and then see how far I can go on it."

After a while, she said, "He called me this morning, just as I was leaving. He told me."

I didn't ask just what he may have told her.

Then she said, "I'll be coming back on the morning train, why don't you come back with us? Spend the rest of the summer with Remy and me." As if reading my thoughts, she added, "Oh, don't worry about him coming there. I said some nasty things to him. He knows I'm really mad at him. He won't come to visit me for a very long time now."

I pressed her hand and said, "It really makes me sad that I have caused this anger and sadness between you and Fred."

She patted my hand and smiled, "Oh, sh sh, life has a way of straightening itself out. Nothing or no one will ever break the love that ties two people together. He will always be my son. And you, my friend, will always be a daughter to me. You know that first minute I met you, I knew you were one of my own."

By the time the train stopped at Sioux Lookout, I promised Gook that I would be joining her on the morning train. When I got to the hotel room, I dumped out my suitcases to see what I actually had in them. I didn't even get a chance to open them at the cabin to see if I had my only good pair of shoes in them. I had on a pair of jeans, tucked-in-shirt, and my old running shoes. But, I found all of my stuff in the suitcases and then, an envelope fell out from one of the pockets inside the lid. Fred must have put it in there. I picked it up and dumped it, there was no letter or even a note. Only some money and money orders. There was two hundred and eighty dollars in total. What was this? My severance pay? An incredible anger filled me that I felt like screaming or just lashing out and punching something as hard as I could! I grabbed a pillow and pressed it to my face and I screamed and sobbed as I sat rocking myself back and forth at the edge of the bed. After a while, I got up, filled the tub and soaked in the hot water for a long, long, time.

* * * *

He had been at the end of his rope! Why was she doing this to him? She seemed to be deliberately leading him on and then she would turn her back on him! There was never an explanation. He was aware that she was embarrassed to talk about what was happening to her. He had even started making excuses as to why she was acting that way, but it just wouldn't work after awhile. Then, that last evening at the trap-line when he had seen Jason in the cabin, he just couldn't take anymore! It didn't take very much to guess what the problem might have been if he left her in such a miserably dark mood and then had come back to hear her laughing and found that it was only because a different man was in there with her! Why didn't she ever laugh like that when he was with her? He had tried to make her laugh, to joke, but all he got were tears and the turn of her head, run and cry episodes. He was tired. He didn't know what else to do!

Now, he was just reacting to the situations he found himself in. He no longer felt in control of anything and everything was just happening to him, all in its own due course. He was being swept down the river again. Where had he gone wrong? What could he have done differently? He hadn't a clue. The situation was driving him crazy! He had even taken to keeping a close watch on Ted. The crazy guy was up to no good. He knew it!

One night, he was just coming around the corner of his cabin when he heard something by the canoe landing. He ran inside the cabin and grabbed the flashlight and snuck down the path toward the lake. Sure enough, there was someone moving around. He crouched down and softly took one step after the other and suddenly flashed the light on the moving shape. It was Ted, and he lit up like a giant alien bug from outer space! He discovered reflector tape from somewhere in Sioux Lookout and he had it taped over his hat band, across the shoulders of his jacket, his sleeves, pants and even around his shoes! Damn duck crap, did he ever look funny!

He burst out laughing and Ted yelled, "Shut off that damned light! I'm trying to hide from that darned Widow Sue! Where you done with your damn canoe anyway!"

What was even more ridiculous was that he was trailing Ted again, over the hills and deep into the bushes beside the store that afternoon of the morning he got off the train at the village. He had been at Bob's place that morning but then the party had moved on across the tracks in the afternoon.

It was there that Karen came in and whispered to him as she passed by the couch where he sat saying, "Got your message. Can't come. Wait for you tonight."

Then she had gone out of the cabin. He did not sent a message to her. Where did she expect to wait for him tonight? What the heck was going on?

The party had then moved to another cabin along the lake by the dock before his own bottles ran out. It was at that time he had gone out to go to the outhouse when he saw Ted's head disappear among the rocks. Wondering what the heck he was doing there, he had quietly followed him down the ravine and deep into the bushes on the other side. Fred saw that Ted was clearly following something and it was just at that moment when Fred swore he saw the head and shoulders of a man in front of Ted that Ted's body was suddenly thrown into fits and he began hitting at the air and thrashing about and he looked totally possessed of the devil himself! It occurred to him that Ted had probably knocked down a wasp's nest in that bush. Fred got out of there quick. It was getting late in the afternoon when he had gone back to his cabin and threw himself on the bed.

The next thing he knew there was Charlie standing there like an Amazon lady in the lamplight! He thought he was dreaming until the door slammed shut! He jumped out of bed and that's when he noticed Karen lying there beside him! When had she come in? Then he had rushed out to chase Charlie, but there was no way on earth he would ever make her believe the truth! And then, just to add pain to the misery, he absolutely didn't know why he had told her that Karen's two small children were his! Well, that did it. That was the end of that. She was gone now. Gone forever!

CHAPTER 23

Several weeks after I had been at the Reserve with Gook, she came back from the store and told me that she had just heard that the tourist guide named Jason from the tourist camp on our lake had disappeared. He had been missing a long time and they still hadn't found him. I said nothing. I couldn't think of a thing to say. How could a person go missing. People didn't just go missing! There was nowhere for people to go in the bush? A guide like Jason didn't just get lost!

Towards the end of the month, I was turning from the sink when Fred walked in. It was such a shock to see him that I dropped the cup I was holding and my knees turned to jelly. Without another glance at me, he walked right by me and went into the living-room where Gook was sitting mending Remy's pants for the tenth time. I was shaking so badly that I did not want him to see me like this! I got out of the kitchen and went into my bedroom where I stayed for the rest of the evening.

Before I went to bed, I heard him leave and Gook came in and sat down beside me. She came to inform me that they had apparently found Karen's body in the bush behind her cabin by her wood-pile yesterday. The people thought that maybe she had slipped on something while she was carrying a log on her shoulder. The log had crushed her head against a rock on the ground. I looked at her but she only glanced at me once before she said that Fred found her that morning when he got off the train from Sioux Lookout. The police had questioned him and everybody in the community but no one knew a thing. That was why he had flown out here. He always came here when he was upset.

My brain was numb, and then I heard myself asking her, "Have they heard anything about Jason?"

She nodded. "Fred says they found his body sometime last week. He had apparently fallen out of his boat and drowned."

I could not see an experienced guide like Jason falling into the water! Someone did something to him! What was I thinking? I lay down and looked at the dark ceiling after Gook left and then later I heard Fred come in. I could tell he was sleeping on the living-room couch. Oh, to be so close to him, yet we were a million miles apart!

Early the next morning, I got up and snuck around in the kitchen fixing myself some coffee and toast. When I anticipated that he would be waking up, I left the kitchen and closed the door to my bedroom again. In a little while Remy came in and crawled into bed with me as he always did in the mornings. Only this time, the bed was already made, so I threw a blanket over his legs as he sat there eating his toast. At these times, we usually talked about different kinds of birds, flies, fish, frogs, snakes and such. Just yesterday morning, he wanted to know what snake pee and poo looked like. I hadn't a clue. I smiled. I could hear Fred coming in and out of the kitchen. I listened to his voice as he spoke with Gook. Then Remy was off again. He wanted to spend some time with Uncle Fred before he left.

Seconds later I heard the front door bang. I thought maybe he had left and I got up and looked out the window. But it was Gook going down the path with her walking stick periodically pointing towards the lake and talking to Remy who was skipping along beside her.

A minute later, the door opened and Fred walked into my bedroom without knocking and said, "We have to talk."

He stood with his back to the door. There was no way for me to leave or to take the liberty of walking away.

I said as coldly as I could, "I have nothing to say to you."

He still had not moved, but his voice was hard, "Maybe you don't, but I've got a lot I want to say to you. And, you are going to listen to me! Since you probably don't even know, I want to tell you what you have been doing to me."

I turned from the window and faced him, "What? What I have been doing to you? I don't need to listen to this!"

I advanced upon him and demanded, "Get out of my way. I am not going to stand here and listen to you any longer!"

His arms came out toward me and I backed away, as he hissed, "You stay there and you listen to me! You took my love and you used it against me. You used my love just so you could torment me! You are selfish and heartless, you take and take, but you give nothing back!"

I was breathing hard now and shaking my head as I replied, "No. No! It is I who gave and gave but it was never enough! My love was never enough, was it? The only thing you saw as proof of my love was a baby. But even that was not enough, was it? Where were you when our baby died inside me? Huh? Where were you? And then, I gave you my love in a million other ways but it still just wasn't enough, was it? All you wanted to do was get me pregnant again. For what? What is one more baby to you when you have others from someone else! No, you wanted me to pay for being different, for not being the same kind of bright hunter and trapper as you are, is that it? I gave you everything a woman could give you but it just wasn't enough! There is just no way you could turn me into a Karen could you? My love just wasn't as good as hers, is that it? Go away! Of all the things that you have taken from me, there is nothing else you can hurt me with further!"

He breathed a big sigh and put his head down a second before he looked at me and said, "I didn't mean what I had said about Karen's children. They are not mine! She had a husband before Big Al and she had been seeing him again and they are his children."

I was near to breaking down and I heard myself shout, "What?"

I couldn't take any more of this!

I struggled to maintain some form of civility as I said in a trembling voice, "Shut up! Don't talk to me anymore about your filth and garbage!"

I blinked rapidly against the sunshine from the window and said the first thing that popped into my mind, perhaps the only thing I could hurt him with, "Murderer! That's what you are! You killed Jason didn't you? For what? Because he was the only person who saw me as a human being?

And what did Karen do to you, eh? Did you catch that whore sleeping with someone else? Did you kill her too?"

That shocked me. My brain shut down and I watched him standing frozen and his face turned grey before he said through clenched teeth, "You are crazy... evil!"

He turned to go and I threw one more question at him, "Then tell me, what really happened to Jason?".

He stared at me for a full minute before he said, "Don't ever come here again. This is my refuge. Mine, do you hear me?"

Then he turned and slammed the door behind him. I stood shaking, looking at the closed door. I nodded. I had heard. Then he was gone. I heard the front door close. So, this is how it would end. I moved to the window and watched him walk away, down the street and around the corner. I didn't realize I was moaning in anguish as the pain in my chest travelled to my throat.

I packed up my bags that afternoon and as I was leaving, Gook came to give me a hug and she pressed an envelope into my hand.

I stood shaking my head, giving back the envelope when she said, "No, it is not from me. Fred said to give it to you, it's yours."

I said nothing. I felt her shoulder bones against my hands. She seemed so frail.

I kissed her forehead and my arms clamped around her and I whispered, "If I knew how much pain and anxiety I would be causing you, I wish I had died then, before all this crap reached you."

Then I turned and went out the door. I headed to the airport in the company of a dozen children or more. Fred had taken Remy for a canoe ride. I didn't even get a chance to say goodbye to the boy. Oh, how my heart ached this day!

On the plane to Nakina, I opened the envelope to find five hundred dollars in it. Where on earth did Fred get that much money?

Where can I go to start all over again? I did not want to go to Thunder Bay. I had been there. I wanted to start brand new in a place I had never lived before.

I went to Winnipeg and managed to find a secretarial job at a construction company. But work wasn't enough. I talked to no one and I knew I had withdrawn into myself again. So, in November, I started to volunteer at the hospital when I wasn't working.

It was just before Christmas, on one of my evenings after work, that I came across Gook in the waiting room. I rushed to her and learned that Remy was okay. Then, it came out that Fred was in the hospital! She was there because of Fred! They had just finished operating on him and he was in critical but stable condition. I was quite shaken and from what I could gather from Gook, Fred had been hauling wood all day to his cabin in the village. His neighbour, Bob, found him that night when he had gone to borrow the axe. A huge pile of logs had rolled down on top of him.

To my questioning look at Gook, she nodded. So, I went to the intensive care unit and saw the bed with his name on it. He was all bandaged up. The shock sent my knees shaking. I hurried out and tried to compose myself before I went back into the waiting room.

I visited him every evening after work and sat by his bed, waiting for him to acknowledge me.

One day, as I was sitting there looking out the window, I became aware that he was awake. His whole face was puffed up and his eyes were mere slits amongst the bandages. But, I knew he was looking at me. They had patched up his skull and he had suffered broken ribs, one arm was in a cast and his left leg was encased in bandages. They stitched up a huge gash down the side of his leg. Not knowing how he would react, I reached out and touched his free hand between the intravenous tubes. I kept my eyes down but I felt no answering pressure from his hand. I told him that Gook had just left but that she would be back later on in the evening and that Remy had also been there. Then he drifted off to sleep again.

A week later, from the time he first saw me, he still had not spoken to me. But, he reached for my hand each time he awoke so I knew he wanted me to stay, but he made no attempt to talk to me. I left each time Gook came in and I'd hear him talking to her in a soft, weak voice. I sat through Christmas day beside his bed. Then, just to keep myself occupied,

I started reading a book to him, a chapter at a time, each time I came. When I first began reading, he turned his face to the wall but I continued. Then each time I came in, he'd hitch himself up in bed and wait.

When work resumed again after the New Year, I came only in the evenings. On one of my visits he had just come back from his shuffling stroll down the hallway and was sitting on the edge of his bed. I knew he would be going home soon. Gook had already gone ahead to prepare the cabin at the village and to wait for him there. He was so gaunt and weak I wondered how Gook would manage.

I set the juice on the table beside him and said, "Here, I brought your favourite drink."

As I sat down on the chair beside the bed and pulled out the book from my handbag to read the last chapter, he asked softly, "Charlie, would you dance with me? I can do the shuffle real good now."

I looked up at him. I couldn't stop the tears that spilled over my cheeks. I wanted so much to reach out and hug him, just to hold him to me. If he had died how could I have gone on in this world without him! Knowing he was safe and my anger at him had been the only two things that had kept me going as I struggled to find a new life for myself.

I put my head down and wiped my eyes and I heard him gently say, "Come here, Charlie."

But, then the nurse came in.

I managed to pull myself together in the time it took the nurse to get Fred back into bed and propped up comfortably before she finally left.

I smiled and pulled up the chair, saying, "Well, do you want to hear the last chapter, or not?"

He nodded and closed his eyes and I began reading. When I had finished, I thought he was asleep and so I began putting on my coat.

As I stood up to leave, I touched his hand and his fingers clasped around mine and he whispered, "Jason, must have seen something or someone, or found out something... I was not there! I could have helped him if I was! He was my friend!"

I immediately said, "Shh, not now. I know. I didn't really think that, what I said. I'm so sorry! But, we'll talk about that some other time, go to sleep now."

His eyes opened and he looked at me, "It wasn't me, Charlie."

I nodded and gripped his hand saying, "I know, I know. I'm sorry I said that, I was just so angry then, I just blindly thought of anything to hurt you with, that was all. I'm sorry, I said that. I know it wasn't you."

Then he whispered, "I did not hurt Karen either. I never hurt anyone, except you."

With his hand keeping a firm grip on mine, his eyes held mine and he said, "The logs. Someone moved the logs."

I stood holding my breathe and my heart was pounding in my ears as I listened to him continue, "I had just come in with the last load. It was dark. I saw one log sticking up at an odd angle and I couldn't figure out how it got like that, and when I pulled it, the whole thing came down."

I was remembering my clothes-line pole at the cabin. No, this was crazy!

I patted his hand and whispered, "Go to sleep, now."

He closed his eyes and I left.

I never saw him after that. I couldn't go to the hospital the next day. I didn't have a telephone and my landlord had been in saying he was coming back to fix the stove later in the afternoon, and I waited. I also had to work the following day so I walked to the corner store to the phone booth and left a message with the nurse to tell Fred that I would not be coming that evening. When I arrived at the hospital the next evening, I found that he had gone home.

I had brushed up on my syllabics during my visits with Gook during the summers and now I wrote to her once in a while. It was now April and she was back at the Reserve. From her letters, I found out that Fred was still in the village and had recovered nicely and was as good as new. She also mentioned that there was something wrong with her heart, but that she had been to see the doctor. Around June, her letters stopped coming and since I had no way to reach her, I called the postal clerk at the store in the village and asked him if he'd ask Fred to be at the store at a certain time that evening when I'd be calling.

That evening when I called, I heard Fred's voice at the other end of the line.

My heart jumped and I had to clear my throat before I said, "Hi. So, are you all mended now?"

His voice came back, "Yeah, I'm fine. Why? Are you thinking of coming back and doing more damage?"

I knew he meant it as a joke but I felt the rush of pain going into my throat before I managed to say, "No. I was calling about Gook. Is she okay? She just suddenly stopped writing."

There was a pause at the other end before I heard him say, "I didn't mean that the way it sounded. It was just, when you used the word mend..."

I interrupted, "Do you know if she's okay?"

His voice came back in a cold tone now, "Yeah, she was here. I took her home the other day. She wasn't feeling well when I left though. She had a cold but she should be all right now. I'll be going back there in a few days. I just came to get my stuff from the cabin here."

Still in an impersonal tone, I asked, "Can you call me around lunch-time at my work number when you get back to her and let me know how she is?"

His response was short, "Yeah, sure."

I gave him the office number where I worked and said goodbye.

It was a week before he called. He said that Gook wasn't feeling well and that she was asking me to come and stay with her for the summer. He sounded like it was almost as an after thought, when he told me that he couldn't stay with her because he was going back to the cabin at the trapline to work as the fishing guide for the tourist camp. He was Jason's replacement. I hung up wondering what I should do.

I quit my secretarial job and took the train home to see my mother. All was well there. By all accounts, the Groundhogs were running wild in the community and the old couple now passed their time sitting on the wooden platform beside the door watching the evening sunset.

Soon after that, I flew out to the Reserve to see Gook. When I arrived I discovered that the Band had moved her to a smaller two bedroom house at the end of the street, next to the Nursing Station. When I entered, a young man came out of the kitchen and his face lit up. I watched his face intently as he laughed and talked excitedly. He looked like Jere. Remy gave me a big hug and a kiss to my cheek before he was off and running down the street to play.

Fred had gone back to the trap-line. He apparently has remained sober for almost a year now.

I had a wonderful summer with Gook. We went fishing in the new aluminum canoe that Remy's family bought for her. At the end of August, Remy went back to Winnipeg and September came. I knew I should have returned to the city long ago, but I couldn't leave Gook. Toward the end of September, I got a secretarial job at the Nursing Station which suited me just fine.

Then one day, as I had finished taking the clothes off the line after work, my heart nearly jumped out of my chest when I found Fred sitting at the kitchen table when I came in. He looked almost back to normal. We spent the evening reminiscing and catching up on news. I noticed that we were very careful that we didn't broach upon subjects that were painful to either of us. Throughout the evening I felt that Fred and I were being drawn closer and closer together, yet the gap was still there; a million miles between us.

I think I am getting very close! They just don't give up do they? My little lost ones are trying to make it home. Maybe in a little while...

CHAPTER 24

Around November at the Nursing Station, the nurse poked her head in the dispensary and said, "Someone here to see you."

I turned around and stood looking at a tall solidly built man. He smiled and immediately the eyes told me it was Ron! Oh my gosh, had he ever changed! He entered the room and we shook hands.

"Hi," I said.

"Hello."

"How you doing?"

"Oh, I'm okay, and you?"

"Oh fine, I guess," I responded.

This was not natural. How phony we both sounded! We burst out laughing. He pulled up a chair and sat down and I did the same.

In the small room our knees almost touched and I said, "So, what are you doing here?"

"Oh, just came to see you."

I smiled, "I mean, what are you doing on the Reserve?"

"Oh, I work at the Band Office. Economic Development."

"How long have you been here?"

"Oh, about a week now. And you?"

"Well, I work here as you found me and I've been living with Gook, I mean Amelia, since July."

"I know. That's how I found out that you were here. Somebody mentioned your name and that you were looking after the old lady. So, I thought I'd come by and say hello."

I tried again. "Is your family here?"

"No. My wife left me last summer. She's married to somebody else

195

now. On the next Reserve, east of here."

"Any kids?"

"No. We never had any kids." He smiled and added, "Maybe that's why she left because she has one now."

Just then Susan, the nurse, came by and Ron said, "Hey, Susan, you know what Channie here used to do for fun when we were kids?"

Now that didn't sound right!

"What do you mean what 'I' used to do? Why don't you say what 'we' used to do?" I said.

Then the laughter started. I sat down at the edge of the counter and watched Ron as he kept the whole clinic entertained for about an hour with stories about our outhouse gang, the Snake-tunnel Skaters and the hell-bent Rump rider of the Toboggans. His hair was still long and he had it tied in a pony-tail at the neck. He had always had long hair, long curly black hair. It was good to listen to Ron telling stories. I hadn't heard him do that in years! He used to keep us entertained with stories when we were teenagers.

When he had gone, Susan remarked, "I never knew Columbo was such a good story teller."

I asked, "Why do you call him Columbo?"

She laughed and said, "Well, the first time he came here, about a year or so ago, he had on an old brown overcoat."

I stood by the window thinking it would be like the one Fred used to have. The one he had lost and never found again. I shook my head. I didn't like where my thoughts were leading.

I hoped tomorrow would be a nice day. Fred was coming to visit.

All through the fall and into the winter, Fred's visits were regular, and we began making a great effort to bridge the gap that had rifted between us the previous year. Gook was there leading the discussion. We spoke of many things, some off-hand, others of a more philosophical nature, others still far into soul searching, and then some evenings just telling jokes and stories. We played cards a lot. There was cribbage, hearts and sometimes we just watched Gook play solitaire.

A few days before Christmas, Fred arrived at Gook's place again. We had not expected to see him, so it was a pleasant surprise when I came home to the sound of his voice in the living-room and hearing Gook quite high and free in her rasping laugh.

I looked at him now and saw the sparkle in his deep brown eyes. He had put on a lot of muscle and he looked great. He became aware that I was watching him and I didn't look away. I figured that if I could ignore his close scrutiny at my body from my feet to the top of my head, he could take me looking at him! He had become a close friend and a friend that I knew I still loved very dearly. He smiled back at me.

That evening, Christmas Eve, we sat around the wood-stove in the dark living-room until after midnight. We sat in the dark so we could see out into the lake a lot better. When Gook went to bed, Fred came and knelt down in front of the chair where I sat facing the living-room window. I had just been admiring the view of the frozen lake in the moonlight when I saw his hand holding something out to me. I needed to see what he was handing me, so he switched the light on beside me.

The light blinded me for a second, then I saw what he had. In his hand was an engagement ring. I took it. On impulse, I picked up the empty box and turned it over and pulled out the guarantee from the case. A receipt fell out with it and I saw the date. He had bought the ring at the time when I was left stranded in the cabin with our dead baby within me! He saw immediately that I remembered and had realized when he had bought the ring. He did not move. My hand clenched the paper a full minute before I pushed it back inside the case. Then he reached for my hand. I did not move as he slipped the ring on my finger. I knew then that this had been a long time in coming and that he must have known that one way or another, I would be beside him again. I reached out for him and we clung to each other. That was the first time I had touched him since I had held his hand at the hospital!

It was around the middle of March when I returned from work and found Ron at Gook's kitchen table. As soon as I walked in he informed me that Gook had to slip out to the grocery store to get some meat for supper.

I realized right away that Gook had another reason because I knew we had more than enough meat in the freezer for supper. I sat down across from him and waited. I watched him fidget.

He kept smoothing down his long curly jet black hair from his forehead before he said, "There is only one way to do this and that is to say it straight out. Are you involved with Fred? If not, can I take you out? I mean, you liked me once, right?"

I looked at him straight in the eyes and shaking my head said, "No, Ron. It never worked that way. Even when we were kids you were my protector, my older brother. You even protected me from people I loved... you'll never know how much I loved Jere at that time! I always looked to you for comfort and protection, but that was all. There can never be anything between us, Ron. I am going to marry Fred."

I looked down at the floor until I felt him move. It was then that I glanced up and a shock ran through me down to my feet! There were those eyes again; very cold, merciless, and almost crazy. In one shake of the head, he was back to normal and he attempted to joke and put me at ease before he got up to leave. I said nothing else as I watched him go out the door.

I talked to Gook but she didn't offer any insight other than that I should remember that if I feed some wild animals they are most likely to come back for more. I said nothing to that.

When Fred came again around the middle of March, Gook was determined that this situation was going to be put to rest once and for all! She was quite healthy and feisty and she sat Fred down at the table across from me and slammed the door behind her. She was off to play Bingo.

We looked at each other for a full minute. Then Fred asked when I had seen Ron last. I hesitated. What was I going to tell him? The truth? I named the date that Ron showed up here at this kitchen.

Fred sat with his head down for the longest time when I told him what Ron had said to me before he took a deep breath and said, "I have to tell you something. You must sit still and not say anything until I have finished. Do you understand? You promise?"

I nodded. What on earth was he about to tell me? I wasn't sure I wanted to hear what was coming.

He took another deep breath and began, "I have had the invisible man, our Weesquachak again at the trap-line several times since you have been here on the Reserve. He seems to think I am some threat even though you are not actually there with me."

I interjected, "What on earth are you talking about? What has he got to do with me?"

He glared at me and said evenly, "Didn't I ask you not to interrupt? Be quiet and listen!"

I took a deep breath and locked my gaze on my clasped hands in front of me on the table as he continued, "It was just before New Years, right after I left here, when I noticed the tracks. That was the very first time that I have known him to come around the trapper's shack in the winter. Well, when I have tracks to go on, then we were on a level playing field. I knew I would get him. Anything that leaves tracks can be caught! Well, after about two days when I knew he was in the area, I made plans to go to Armstrong. By all my tracks and behaviour I made it look like that. Only I turned around about ten miles away and made my way back through high ground and as I approached the cabin from the inland peninsula, I noticed the fresh tracks. I tracked him right to the cabin. A blizzard had started to blow late in the evening, but I knew every foot of the land so it was no effort for me to reach the cabin. It was then, that as I approached the cabin from behind the wood-pile that I became aware that there was a man just in front of me. The snow was coming down thick and heavy that night and I was only about six feet behind him when he pushed the cabin door open. You know that four-foot stick I always have leaning against the door that I use to whack my snowshoes to get the snow off? Well, I picked that up and hit him on the back of the head. He went down inside the cabin. I stepped over him in the dark and lit a candle. He was just coming to when I yanked him up by the collar and tied his hands behind him and tied him to the bed-frame and sat him up on the bench. It was then that I took a good look at him. He wore a balaclava over his face. All that was showing was his mouth and eyelids. He was looking straight at me when I yanked off his mask.

And, it was Ron."

My heart almost leapt into my mouth! "Ron! What? Why?"

A long, long time passed where we just looked at each other, minds going through the past months and years. Then after a while, in a very sick way, I acknowledged that it could have been him. The message I got from Fred's eyes told me that he had no doubt that our invisible man and his attempted murderer was none other than our friendly gentle Ron.

My next question was, "What did he say?"

He understood my questioning gaze and continued, "I told him that I would keep his hands tied until I took him to the police. Then, he told me that he had only just arrived to ask me if he could court you, like, see you... kind of thing? Then, he said that if I hurt him in any way, he would say that he had seen me coming down the path where they found Karen dead that morning. He was determined to accuse me of murdering Karen if I ever accused him of attempting to hurt me or you or anyone else. He also said that he would testify that I had tried to kill you that night on the lake when the whole community had witnessed the scene. He seemed very intent that no bad word should come to you about him. In return for my silence about my suspicions, he would keep his mouth shut about me and Karen. So, I must tell you about that night. I got off the evening train at that tourist camp about three miles west of the village, and I virtually spent the night huddled by the railroad tracks, trying to figure out how I was going to approach you. You see, I had chickened out. I heard you were back in the village and I just could not get off and not see you... and I was just not ready to face you just yet... you understand? Anyway, the next morning, I walked the three miles to the village and you know Karen's cabin is the first one at the end. It was then, that I found her. I knew something was amiss as soon as I approached her cabin. I don't care what anyone else thought of her, but to me she was always a friend. She always took very careful watch over her children and I saw her most of the time only as a friend. Only, I could not say anything since I didn't officially get off the train, you understand? And, I didn't know anything more than what everyone else knew. Anyway, there it was. Ron was now blackmailing me, saying that he could say I was the murderer and that he was a witness to the whole scene. I felt that I just did not have a choice. Keep quiet or answer to a whole lot of questions that were going to cost me a whole lifetime and a lot of suspicion... and you! I just could not afford to lose you forever on a false charge of murder. That was the last thing I needed to come between us! As to all my suspicions about Ron, well, I still have absolutely no proof whatsoever. I don't know if he was telling the truth that he had only just arrived to talk to me, because then, the snow had covered up all the footprints. So, I cut him loose with a warning that if I ever saw him on my territory again, I would hang his you-know-what right beside the beavers'!"

I put my head down and let the information sink in. I could not decide whether Ron would take this as a threat for the future or whether it would put an end to past harassment. There was no way to know. I looked at Fred and as honesty and openly as I knew how, I told him that I believed him. I also had my doubts that Ron would be that clever. I was more inclined to believe that he had only just arrived to get Fred's permission to see me. I looked at Fred, we had come an awful long way and I hoped that our paths would stay merged from this time on. He was still sober after a year and a half. I had remembered to reach out without fear and he was right there with me.

Fred and I got married at the church on the Reserve in the spring. As any wedding draws a crowd for a celebration, we emerged from the church and found all the people lined up outside to shake our hands to wish us well. Halfway through the crowd, Ron suddenly stepped in front of me. Without a pause, he pulled me into his arms and hugged me and then turned to Fred. At that moment I sensed that the world stood still. They seemed totally oblivious to everyone around them and the tension was almost visible. Whatever had happened between them obviously had gone beyond me. Their eyes bore into each other, then Ron moved. He bowed slightly to Fred, then turned around on his heel and disappeared through the crowd. A raven swooped down over his head, squawking above the crowd. We never saw Ron again.

In the stillness of the dawning light, I folded my wings close to my body and welcomed the pungent odour of my wolf scent. It is the sense of smell that first invades my present form in the process of transformation. It is the smell of man that I find most abhorrent when I move from the wolf into the shape of a man... brrrr! The fur on the back of my neck literally stands on end! Only my stealth and senses shift when I move from dog to wolf. My mind changes the most from any form to that of the raven. I am anything I want to me. I am he. I am she. I am it. I am. I shall rest now. A well-earned rest. Goodbye my lost ones, for you are now found. They should thank me that they have found each other.

It was early June when we landed at Clay Lake. I had the little black puppy that Fred had presented me with on our wedding day. I held it against my chest as we approached the cabin at the trap-line and I saw that it had changed. There was a new fish-cleaning shed beside the dock with screening all around. And up at the point, I saw a screened-in shade with a picnic table nestled between the trees. The air smelled wonderfully fresh. The birds chirped in the trees and several squirrels came chasing each other across the path in front of us. The brush had been cleared all around, leaving the trees room for their branches to spread to the sun. There was no grass to grow but the ground was covered with low ground plants with their leaves weaving a green carpet six to eight inches from the earthy soil.

I walked up the path and there was the cabin in front of me. It now had a porch with bug-screen windows on the top half. And there, beside a large covered wood-shed, with steps leading up to it, was a clothes-line platform with another higher step in the corner for easy reach to the pulley.

I glanced back to see a big smile on Freddy's face. How I truly loved this man! He held the cabin door open for me and I went in, stepping onto a "welcome home" mat by the door. The log walls had been covered with wood panelling and the floor had been covered with linoleum. A birch-bark canoe with carpeted flooring came immediately to mind. Then my eyes settled on two rows of books on a shelf above the bed.

I glanced at him, "Books?"

He threw his head back and laughed.

He said, "Well, you got me hooked on books when you read that one to me in the hospital."

As I stood there looking at the work he had put into this place, at each loving detail, I knew that words had their place and deeper knowledge was better left unsaid.

Fred came up from behind and put his arms around me and whispered, "Welcome home, Charlie."

Printed and bound
in Boucherville, Quebec, Canada by
MARC VEILLEUX IMPRIMEUR INC.
in April, 2000